The Wise Men of Helm

Daddy,

Peter Oberfest gave us this book a few years ago. When I was a kid Polish jokes were the Norm.

I gather that Al Rosenblatt loves these stories as well.

With love.

Eliot

D1299602

The Wise Men of Helm

and their Merry Tales

SOLOMON SIMON

Illustrated by

LILLIAN FISCHEL

BEHRMAN HOUSE, PUBLISHERS

THE WISE MEN OF HELM

Copyright renewed, 1973, by Mrs. Solomon Simon

Copyright, 1945, by Solomon Simon

Originally published in Yiddish as "Di Helden fun Chelm."

Copyright, 1942, by Solomon Simon

Translated into English by Ben Bengal and David Simon

Printed in the U. S. A.

Published by Behrman House, Inc., 11 Edison Place, Springfield, 07081

Library of Congress Cataloging-in-Publication Data

Simon, Solomon
    [Heldn fun Khelm. English]
    The Wise Men of Helm and Their Merry Tales / Solomon Simon:
illustrated by Lillian Fischel.
    ISBN-13: 978-0-87441-469-1
    1. Jews--Poland--Chelm (Chelm)--Fiction. 2. Jewish wit and humor.
    I. Title.
    PJ5129.S48H4213 1995
    892.4 35--dc20   95-36120
                                              CIP

Some people say that the Wise Men of Helm are fools. Don't you believe it. It's just that foolish things are always happening to them.

Contents

In the beginning

DEEP IN THE FORESTS OF POLAND, QUITE HID-den from all the world, lay the little town of Helm. The people who lived there were Jews, and like all other Jews, they had long beards and curly side-locks around their ears. They wore long, shiny, black coats that reached to their ankles and striped prayer-shawls with thick fringes. Just like Jews all over the world at that time. Yet, frankly, there was something peculiar about the Helmites, some-thing odd about the way they did things. Truth to tell, they weren't really quite like other people.

There was that winter, for instance, a cold, bitter winter, when the Helmites had no fire-wood to warm their homes. They suffered much through the long months, and, deter-mined that such a thing should never again happen in Helm, the very next year they built a high brick wall all around the town to keep out the cold.

Then there's that other story about how they decided to invite the most famous organist of the great city of

Warsaw to play for them. They hadn't ever heard an organ before, so they awaited him with eager anticipation, never realizing that there wasn't a single organ in all of Helm.

It was after this that people began to wonder about the Helmites. They said they were just fools. Then they asked one another how so many fools came to collect in one place, and therein too lies a tale:

Once upon a time an angel, carrying a sackful of foolish souls back to heaven for repair, lost his way in a storm and flew over Helm. The town, as you know, lies in a valley, completely surrounded by high mountains. On the topmost peak of the highest mountain stood a tall, pointed tree. Suddenly, as the angel struggled through the storm, the bottom of the sack caught and tore on the tree-top, and alas, all the poor, damaged souls spilled out of the ripped sack, rolled down the mountain side into Helm and there they stayed from that day on.

But the foolishness of Helm was so fabulous that it couldn't be explained away by just one tale, so here's another: Once a great wind blew over the town, a wild, swirling wind, sweeping with it a stream of air from the strange isle of Abdera. Now it is well-known among certain scientists who spend most of their lives bothering

with these things that the air of Abdera has a very unusual quality. One whiff of it makes a man a simpleton for life. And no sooner did the Helmites begin to breathe this air than they and their children and their children's children all became fools.

Naturally, the wise men of Helm never dreamed that the world looked upon them as fools until one day Berel the Beadle left the town to journey to Shedlitz. There, for the first time, a Helmite learned what the world thought of Helm. Hardly able to believe his ears, Berel hurried home in alarm to report to Mottel the Mayor.

Frantically, Mottel called a Town Meeting, and for seven days and seven nights, the leading citizens of Helm thought and thought and thought. On the seventh night of the seventh day, when their brows were as wrinkled as prunes, Mottel suddenly shot up from his seat, exclaiming, "Why didn't I think of it before! It's simple. We Helmites aren't fools. It's just that foolish things are always happening to us." Thereupon a sigh of relief arose from the assembly and all the brows became smooth again. Delighted with this wise explanation, the Helmites immediately decided to send forth a messenger to proclaim it to the world.

But for this important mission, no ordinary Helmite

would do—only the cleverest youth in town. Meetings were held to make the selection, discussions took place and finally a contest was announced with Mottel the Mayor as judge. Day in and day out, the young men of Helm appeared before Mottel who found them all so filled with true Helmite wisdom that he was sorely tried to choose from amongst them. However, when Gimpel the son of Mendel appeared before him, he knew that here at last stood the true representative of Helm.

For was it not about Gimpel that this story was told? Once while eating a slice of white bread thickly spread with gleaming yellow butter, it slipped from his hands and fell to the floor. Now, it's pretty well known that when a slice of bread falls, it always lands on the buttered side. But Gimpel's didn't, and when he was asked why, he brightly replied, "It's obvious—the butter was spread on the wrong side."

Now give heed to the extraordinary way in which Gimpel the son of Mendel answered the Mayor's questions:

"Why is the sea salty?" asked Mottel.

Without a moment's hesitation came Gimpel's reply, "Naturally, because of the herring. The herring is salted—and that makes the water salty, too."

Pleased, the Mayor pricked up his ears and put the second question, "If the distance from Helm to Shedlitz is four miles, what is the distance from Shedlitz back to Helm?"

"Eight miles," came Gimpel's prompt reply.

"And can you tell us why?" asked Mottel the Mayor, smiling eagerly.

"Certainly," Gimpel answered. "It's simple. There are four months from Chanukah to Passover and eight months from Passover back again to Chanukah."

Now the Mayor grinned with pleasure and flung the final question, "Why are summer days long and winter days short?"

In a flash, Gimpel answered, "That's easy, in the summer, the days expand because of the heat, and in the winter, they contract because of the cold."

The Mayor nearly jumped out of his skin with delight— even for Helmites, this was truly a great mind.

Soon, attired in the best the town had to offer, Gimpel was sent forth into the world to proclaim the message of Helm. Years passed and when he finally returned and recounted the amazing way he had been received by the peoples of all the strange lands through which he had journeyed, the Helmites then and there decided that the

world was unquestionably inhabited by a pack of fools. All except Helm, of course.

6 Now in the course of his travels, Gimpel made one important discovery. Each and every town wherever he went boasted a Town Record in which was preserved the chronicle of all its doings. Yet Helm whose wisdom far outshone all others had nothing of the sort. Here was a matter that had to be remedied, and quickly. A Town Meeting was hurriedly called and for seven days and seven nights the leading citizens of Helm thought and thought and thought, and at last they decided. You'll never guess what they decided! It was just that Helm too must have a Town Record!

Now why do I tell you all this? Not many years ago, whilst rummaging amongst some old papers, I accidentally came upon a curious document, worn and yellowed and covered over with dust. It was none other than the long-lost Record of Helm! I read it, fascinated. Then, feeling as I do, that the people of Helm would have wanted you to know the truth about them in all their great wisdom, it occurred to me that I ought to set down their story for you. Without delay, I commenced transcribing it and now I give it to you in my own words.

The watermill that wouldn't work

FOR MANY YEARS, THE HELMITES KEPT TO themselves, venturing forth only twice a year to bring their grain to nearby Shedlitz for milling at the big watermill by the river.

Now, once it happened on a fine spring day that five wagons piled high with grain were going from Helm to Shedlitz. Over the hills and through the valleys rolled the wagons.

Five wagons, five horses, and eleven wise men of Helm carting grain from Helm to Shedlitz. Five tall, thin Helmites walking with the horses, leading them by the bit, and five short, fat Helmites sitting high up on the wagon-seats, holding the reins. For each wagon, one horse and two Helmites. Altogether, five wagons, five horses, and ten wise men of Helm.

But lo, there was an eleventh who was the wisest of them all—Gimpel, now the foremost citizen of Helm. In the leading wagon, reclining on a pile of hay, Gimpel traveled like a true prince.

On the way, the Helmites stopped to rest. All through the journey, Gimpel had been thinking his head off. He now arose. Quoth he:

"O Helmites, pray tell me, why do we bring our wheat to Shedlitz for grinding?"

"A very wise question." The Helmites turned to each other in awe.

"We bring our wheat to Shedlitz for grinding because there is a watermill in Shedlitz and none in Helm," Gimpel expounded sagely.

"True," nodded the others, "very true."

"Of course, it's true!" declared Gimpel. "And now, tell me," he continued, beaming at his own cleverness, "shouldn't we build a watermill in Helm?"

"What a wonderful idea!" nodded the Helmites.

"Then we'll build one!" shouted Gimpel, enthusiastically.

"Nothing will stop us!" cried the Helmites.

Upon arriving in Shedlitz, the very first thing they did after unloading their grain was to scrutinize the watermill from all angles. They looked at it frontwards, backwards, sidewards and also from above and below. They saw how it stood on the river bank where watermills always stand.

They watched the enormous wheel churning the water as it was pushed by the current of the stream. Then, hurrying back to Helm as fast as their horses could carry them, they immediately called a Town Meeting and revealed the new project to their townsfolk.

The Helmites were overjoyed. "What a great idea! Helm to have its own watermill! Hurrah, no more trips to Shedlitz, a town full of simpletons!" Excitement ran so high that Mottel the Mayor exclaimed extravagantly, "Helmites! We must spare no expense. Our watermill must be the best, the biggest, and the most beautiful watermill ever built!"

The people shouted their approval. Not to be outdone by Mottel the Mayor, Gimpel was inspired by another idea. He cried out:

"Yes, Helmites, our watermill must be like no other watermill. It must be a tribute and a monument to the superior wisdom of Helm. Therefore it must not be low down in the valley—it shall be on the topmost mountain peak where it can be seen by everyone from far and wide. Let our enemies see it and burst with envy," he ended, waving his arms wildly.

So the Helmites built their watermill on a mountaintop and when it was finished it was indeed a sight to behold.

The roof was made of tin and painted red. The big water-wheel was made of the finest oak and painted green. So that the walls might be as perfect as possible, they were made without a single break or window. The millstones were brought all the way from far-off Leipzig. Nor did they forget the weathercock on the roof—not the Helmites.

The last nail had been hammered in. The mill was complete. Amidst great fanfare and joyous shouting, the first wagons of wheat were brought to the mill to be ground. With his own hands, Gimpel, the wisest man in all Helm, poured the grain into the great bins. Then he stuffed his ears with cotton and so did all the other Helmites. Finally he pushed the lever that controlled the waterwheel, closed his eyes tight, waiting with screwed-up face for the first thunderclap from the turning wheel. He stood there and waited for the wheel to turn and the cogs to clatter, for the millstones to grind and for a cloud of flour-dust to float to heaven. But—strange! The wheel did not turn, the cogs did not clatter, the millstones did not grind—and there was no cloud of dust. The mill remained as silent and motionless as a picture on paper.

The Helmites pulled the cotton out of their ears, opened their eyes, stared, and wondered. Gimpel wondered too. How odd! He couldn't understand why the mill wouldn't

work! The best architects in Helm had drawn the plans, and the best workmen had carried them out. Then why wouldn't the mill work?

The leading citizens of Helm called a Town Meeting. The architects came, the masons and the carpenters. They brought their papers, their pencils, their rulers and their plumb-lines. They examined the mill. They scrutinized every brick and board and nail. Everything was in order. The doors were in place, there were knobs on the doors and locks under the knobs. There were keys in the locks. The millstones each had its hole in the center. There was the weathervane on the roof, as it should be.

"The mill must turn!" decided the architects after grave thought.

"Try again!" commanded Mottel the Mayor.

Once again Gimpel pushed the lever but again nothing happened.

Then Shloime, one of Helm's leading scientists, smacked his forehead and exclaimed:

"I know why the mill doesn't work! There isn't any light inside. Walls are indeed beautiful when they are perfectly smooth, but our mill has no windows. And without windows, it is dark."

"Well, and what if it *is* dark inside the mill?" asked Berel the Beadle.

With elaborate gesturing of his thumb, Shloime the Scientist patiently explained, "Wherever darkness is, evil spirits abide. Since the mill is dark, there are goblins inside, and the goblins of course are holding back the waterwheel."

"Naturally," Gimpel turned to Berel scornfully, "even a fool could understand that." Berel really *didn't* understand, but not wishing to display his ignorance in the presence of all these Helmite wise men, he kept his mouth shut.

"Pour the light of day into the mill!" commanded Mottel.

So the wise people of Helm seized buckets, casks, barrels

and sacks, and carried them outside into the sunlight. The womenfolk began catching the sunbeams in their sacks, then quickly, quickly, they tied them up, slung them over their shoulders, ran into the mill, opened them, and poured the sunbeams into the darkness of the mill.

The men carried in barrels full of sunlight on their shoulders. The children dragged buckets full of light into the mill. How they all worked and labored to get the sunlight inside! Sacks packed full of sunbeams, pails full, whole barrels full of sunlight. But still the mill remained dark.

Declared Shloime the Scientist:

"Alas, this won't do. We must tear the roof off the mill."

So they tore off the roof and the mill was flooded with sunshine and light, but the waterwheel still did not turn, the gears did not clatter, and the millstones did not grind.

Once again the Helmites called a Town Meeting. They thought and they thought—there was more thinking that day in Helm than in all of the rest of the world put together—but to no avail. Finally, in desperation, they went back to the mill and again examined every screw and every cog. They measured. They scribbled figures. They found everything as it should be. Still the mill didn't work.

Berel the Beadle suddenly got an idea, but it seemed so foolish to him, he was reluctant to mention it. Finally, it popped out in spite of himself. "It seems to me a water-mill needs water," he ventured, timidly. At this, Mottel, Gimpel and Shloime looked at him with utter scorn, but after a while it was decided to give even this ridiculous idea a try.

"Helmites, pour water upon the wheel," commanded Mottel.

The people fell into a long line that stretched from the mill on the mountain to the stream in the valley. At one end, men, women and children drew water from the river, and at the other end, they splashed it over the mill wheel. But still—all in vain. The great wheel did not turn, the gears did not clank, and the stones did not grind. The mill refused to work.

Just then a stranger passed, looked at the beautiful watermill on the top of the mountain and saw the Helmites with their pails and tubs. Bursting with laughter, he called out:

"O wise men of Helm, if you want the watermill to work, build it by a river with the wheel against the stream."

All the wise men of Helm scoffed.

"Listen to the silly ideas of this fool of a stranger! Build it by a river! What a notion! Pouring light into the mill didn't work. Tearing off the roof didn't work. Pouring water over the wheel didn't work either, and he thinks that something so simple as placing the mill by a river will help!"

The stranger left, bent over double with laughter.

Still the mill didn't work.

So another Town Meeting was called. It was decided that the climate of Helm was not suitable for watermills. But things were getting serious. To build the mill, the last kopek had been squeezed out of Helm, all the lands were mortgaged and now, since the mill wouldn't work, the Helmites didn't even have any flour. But there is an old Jewish proverb: God provides the weaver with thread and the beggar with bread. And it was just at that time that a rich Jewish miller from a neighboring town appeared in Helm with a strange proposition. But that's another story, so we may as well begin another chapter.

No one can fool a Helmite

EARLY ONE MORNING, A MILLER ARRIVED IN Helm, climbed the mountain, and began to examine the mill.

Around and around walked the miller, followed by all the Helmites, mouths agape. They walked around and around, after him, eager to know what his business was.

The strange miller casually remarked, "A lovely mill!"

"Of course it's a lovely mill," echoed the Helmites.

"But," continued the miller, stroking his beard, "the waterwheel doesn't turn, the cogs don't clatter, and the millstones don't grind."

"True," the Helmites nodded.

The stranger went on:

"The mill will never work. After all, it's a watermill, and a watermill must be built near a stream, with the great wheel against the current."

"We've heard that foolishness before," sneered Gimpel, "but it isn't true. We Helmites are convinced that the mill doesn't turn because the climate of Helm is not suitable for watermills."

The stranger looked sharply at Gimpel, the wisest man in Helm, and noticed that the Helmites, like so many sheep, were nodding at Gimpel's every word.

Thought the miller:

"When in Helm, do as the Helmites do. If one talks to a child, one talks like a child, and if one deals with a Helmite, one reasons like a Helmite."

So the miller said to Gimpel:

"Yes, I too have heard that the climate of Helm is not suitable for watermills. But you Helmites own a mountaintop that is an excellent place for a windmill."

"There is the watermill on our mountaintop," said Gimpel.

"Sell me the watermill," said the miller, "and I will rebuild it into a windmill."

"Sell the watermill!" Gimpel shuddered. "No! We have labored too long and too hard to build it."

The Helmites nodded in agreement.

"But it's of no use to you!" said the miller.

"Nonsense," retorted Gimpel. "The mill is beautiful. It can be seen for miles around. We can look at it and admire it."

"You could look at a windmill, too," said the strange miller.

This thought so confused and bewildered the Helmites that they immediately decided to call a Town Meeting to give the matter their fullest and weightiest consideration. For seven days and seven nights they pondered until finally they decided to allow the strange miller to address them. Whereupon he arose and said:

"Sell me the watermill which I intend to rebuild into a windmill. That will give you a chance to pay off the mortgages on your land, and even have a little something left over for herring and onions three times a week."

The poor folk of Helm looked pleadingly at Gimpel, who now rose thoughtfully to answer the miller:

"I have a plan."

"He has a plan, he has a plan," chorused the Helmites eagerly. "Let us hear the plan!"

"Yes, let's hear the plan," sighed the miller.

Gimpel turned to the Helmites:

"The miller likes our mountain because the mountaintop is an excellent place for a windmill. But we don't care to part with our watermill. Therefore, let's push our mill to one side, and there'll be plenty of room left on the mountaintop for both."

"Now, there's a brain for you!" rejoiced the Helmites.

The miller shrugged his shoulders and remained silent.

But he decided to stay in Helm to see what would happen.

20   The very next morning, the Helmites gathered on the mountaintop and began preparing to push the watermill aside. They removed their coats, piled them on the ground, rolled up their sleeves, spat upon their palms, and—began to push.

They pushed and pushed and pushed. They pushed till they puffed for breath. They pushed till they were drenched in sweat. They pushed so hard, they didn't even

know they weren't budging it an inch. So engrossed were they in their labor that they had eyes for nothing else.

A thief, who happened to pass just then, noticed the pile of clothes with no one guarding it, so he took pity on the coats and carried them off.

All day long the good folk continued to push and push and push. When the sun began to set, Mottel commanded:

"Stop! We've worked long enough! Let's see how far we've pushed the mill."

The chill of evening having descended on the mountaintop, the Helmites went to look for their coats. They looked here, they looked there, they looked everywhere. There was no sign of a coat anywhere.

"Ha!" exclaimed Gimpel gleefully. "That's Helm for you! When we do something, we do it right! We've pushed the mill so far that we can't even see our coats. Send for the miller. Now he has plenty of room for his windmill."

The miller came, looked at the mill, looked at the weary Helmites, and remarked hopelessly:

"The mill stands exactly where it stood before. You haven't moved it an inch."

"Then where are our coats?" asked Gimpel angrily.

"How should I know where your coats are?" replied the miller. "Maybe someone stole them," he added.

"Listen to the fool," snapped Gimpel. "Who would need so many coats? No one can wear more than one!"

"Now I know what they meant when they told me about the Helmite who was going to Warsaw and his wagon died, his horse fell apart and his whip became lame in one leg," retorted the miller, and departed forthwith.

22

How the millstones drowned

AFTER **THE DEPARTURE OF THE STRANGE** miller, Helm became poorer than ever. Day in and day out, the gloomy townsfolk had nothing to eat but plain dry bread and watery potato soup. It filled their stomachs but still they were hungry. The Helmites were unhappy. No longer did they sing and laugh. Only the crickets chirped in their holes every night.

"Tsirk! tsirk! tsirk!" sang the crickets: "Dry bread and potato soup—and soon that too will be gone."

Hungry and sad, the Helmites were sitting in their watermill. In came Mottel the Mayor with a plan. Seeing the gloomy, dejected faces of his people, he reflected:

"Things have gone from bad to worse. I must do something to make them laugh."

Thereupon, Mottel, who was one of the most dignified men in all Helm, got down on all fours and began to crawl over the floor, seeming to peer and search in every nook and cranny.

"Mottel, what are you looking for?" they cried in astonishment.

Replied Mottel, "I see that everyone lost heart, so I'm trying to find it."

The Helmites burst into laughter. When Mottel saw that they were more cheerful, he jumped onto the great millwheel and began to speak:

"Helmites, take heart! I have a plan that will deliver us from poverty and want."

"The plan, the plan!" shouted the Helmites eagerly.

"Then listen with both ears!" Mottel said to them. "True, the mill is beautiful and it would be a shame to sell it. But it's no good for grinding. So why not sell the millstones, which are no good for anything but grinding? With the money we'll redeem our mortgaged fields and become prosperous again."

"Good, good!" acclaimed the Helmites.

Mottel continued: "Taking the millstones out of a mill is easier than taking a hair out of milk, and takes less time than eating a herring. Since the mill is on top of the mountain we can roll the stones down the hill into the valley and straight to the market."

No sooner said than done. Twenty men and forty boys set to work on the millstones. They unscrewed bolts, loosened boards, and pulled out all the nails. Some of the

Helmites were hammering, and the rest of the Helmites were sawing, and after much toiling and sweating they pried the two stones loose.

After the millstones had been loosened, Mottel climbed onto a ladder and shouted:

"Careful, Helmites! Out of the way there! Push! Push! A little more! A little harder! Ho! Hup! The millstone—whup!" And away went the first millstone.

It rolled down the mountain. Down, down it rolled, straight into the town itself, from the town into the valley, from the valley, whush!—right into the river and no more! The millstone sank deep into the river—and that was the end of the millstone.

The Helmites were dumbfounded—how could the millstone be gone already?

But Mottel, refusing to permit himself to become too disturbed by this, quickly said:

"The millstone fell into the river and drowned. Too bad. But don't get upset. We still have another millstone. And I have a plan so that we won't lose that one too."

The Helmites listened to the Mayor's new plan:

"As everyone knows, in a millstone there is a hole. Our beadle will squeeze his head into the hole. Then we'll roll the stone down the mountain. If this stone too should

happen to fall into the river, then the beadle will remove his head from the hole, come to the surface and let us know where the stone is."

"A brilliant idea," the Helmites agreed.

"Not so brilliant for me," blurted out Berel the Beadle. Everyone looked at him a little sadly, for it had been suspected that he wasn't quite possessed of true Helmite wisdom. But since it is well-known that beadles who do all the menial tasks in the Synagogue are really the servants of the whole community, Berel had no choice but to obey. With a sigh of resignation, he squeezed his head into the hole in the millstone.

The Helmites gave the second millstone a shove. Stone and beadle began to roll down the mountain. From the mountain into the town. From the town into the valley. From the valley right into the river.

"Whush, whush," gurgled the river.

The Helmites stood on the bank and waited. Soon the beadle would swim to the surface and show them just where the stone had sunk. But—

They waited an hour. Two hours. Three hours. One day. Two days. But the beadle did not swim to the surface and did not point out the spot where the millstone was.

When the Helmites saw that the beadle had no intention of returning, they sent messengers to all the surrounding towns to proclaim in the market places that, if a short, thin Jew with a pointed, red beard was seen trying to sell a millstone that he carried around his neck, he should be arrested at once and returned to Helm for stealing the town's property.

The greedy red lobster

ALAS, THE MILLSTONES WERE NEVER FOUND, but as the Helmites say, God watches over orphans and simpletons, and a few days later, Berel the Beadle turned up on the opposite bank of the river, a little damp, but otherwise none the worse for his ducking.

But Helm itself still fared poorly. The townsfolk were as poor as blind beggars. And all they had to eat was potatoes.

On Sunday the Helmites ate potatoes, on Monday potatoes, and on Tuesday and Wednesday more potatoes: on Thursday and Friday they ate potatoes again: but on the Sabbath, for a change, they ate potato pudding.

All Helm lived on potatoes—and dreamed of a piece of herring. Speaking of herring, of which the Helmites had none, they spent their days figuring out how they'd prepare it if they had any. First they'd give it a thorough washing, then they'd soak it in boiling water. After the soaking, they'd remove the scales and carefully skin it. Then the Helmite would take a sharp knife and slice the herring into thin pieces, after which he'd assemble it all over again, so skillfully that the fish would seem to be whole and untouched. Then, after slicing an onion into thin ribbons, he'd make a frame of it around the herring. And last, as the crowning touch, he'd lovingly sprinkle pepper and vinegar over everything.

Then the lean and hungry Helmites would go on to dream of eating it. Naturally, you couldn't eat herring with anything but a thick chunk of fresh black bread, and, smacking their lips, they'd tell how in Paradise God gives all good, pious folk black bread and herring three times a day.

One day, Gimpel himself, leading citizen of Helm, was seated on an empty herring barrel in the market-place. He too was dreaming of the good old days when purses were heavy with silver and wondering how he could change the climate of Helm so that the mill would work.

Inspired by a most fragrant whiff from the empty barrel on which he was sitting, an idea suddenly flashed through his mind:

"Helmites, I have a plan! Let's buy five barrels of salted red herring and five barrels of salted white herring. Then we'll dump all the fish into the Helm River so that they can multiply and increase. Next year we'll hire some

fishermen who'll catch as much herring as we want. But we'll be smart—we'll make sure to leave a few fish in the river to multiply and increase again and in this way we can have herring forever."

"A marvellous idea," responded one of the Helmites, "truly worthy of the foremost citizen of Helm. Now maybe that Helmite brain of yours can figure out where we're to get the money to buy the herring. After all, the mill won't work, the millstones are lost and we've already mortgaged all our land."

"Poof," Gimpel dismissed him with a wave of his hand. "You call that a problem. We'll take out a second mortgage."

Once again, the Helmites were awed and reassured in their faith in Gimpel's superior wisdom. And for days thereafter they went around repeating to one another the magic words, *"Poof! Second Mortgage!"*

And that was just what the citizens of Helm did. They took out second mortgages on their land, bought five barrels of salted red herring and five barrels of salted white herring, and one night when the moon was full, all the townsfolk assembled on the bank of the Helm River. There, amidst elaborate ceremonies, each Helmite took his turn in tossing a pair of salted herring into the river,

starting with Gimpel and Mottel and ending with Berel the Beadle, in the order of their wisdom.

Patiently, the good folk waited a year and a day—then another day for good measure. They hired a band of fishermen, went to the river, and watched eagerly as the nets were thrown out. Gradually the nets settled upon the water and then slowly sank. All Helm waited with gaping mouths.

Now the fishermen were dragging in the nets, panting and sweating as they labored. Finally the nets were in— empty, absolutely empty. Nothing inside but a few bits of weed and a little mud—one could hardly put any onions around that.

So the fishermen threw out their nets again. Again they labored long and hard, and this time all they got for their pains was an old, torn boot. Still nothing that would be very tasty with onions. As for the herring, there was not a sign.

Gimpel, furious with rage, cried out:

"Throw out the nets again! The fish must be there!"

The fishermen obeyed. They labored a whole day but did not catch enough to feed a fly. Finally, just before nightfall, their efforts were rewarded when they caught a huge, red lobster with tremendous claws, the likes of

which had never been seen before. Breathing hard, they hauled the monster onto the sand.

Stunned, Gimpel stared bewilderedly for a few moments. Then, collecting his wits, with which you'll remember he was considerably endowed, and choking with indignation, he finally managed to stammer, "There Helmites, is your culprit. There is the thief. Look closely at this ugly monster, red all over, a sign that it is gorged with the blood of our helpless herring."

"Destroy the horrible beast!" stormed the Helmites. "Tear it apart limb from limb!"

"Wait," interrupted Pinya the Philosopher of Helm. "Who ever heard of tearing a lobster apart. One speaks

of tearing a herring apart, but never a lobster," he ended with an emphatic twist of the thumb.

"Then chop the wicked creature up!"

"No, that won't do either," declared Pinya. "One speaks of chopped liver, but never of chopped lobster."

"Then roast it!" cried one of the Helmites.

"No, that's not right either. You roast a goose or a duck, and often meat, but never a lobster," uttered Pinya the Philosopher.

"Then what shall we do with the thief? How shall we punish him?"

Pinya thought a moment, for after all it would not be seemly for a Helmite philosopher to render a snap judgment, then slowly spoke as follows:

"Horrible is the crime, horrible shall be the punishment. What is a more frightful death than drowning? In the time of Noah when God decided to punish the whole, wicked world, did he not send a flood upon it? Let this fiendish glutton be drowned!"

"Just as you say, so shall it be," rejoined the Helmites.

"Drown the murderer of our innocent herring!"

In recognition of his wise verdict, Pinya the Philosopher was unanimously given the honor of seizing the lobster and tossing it into the deepest part of the river. And that's how the Helmites took revenge on the greedy red lobster.

The Helmites

capture the moon

ALTHOUGH THE LOBSTER RECEIVED HIS JUST punishment and Pinya the Philosopher had his moment of glory, nonetheless the stomachs of Helm were still rumbling with hunger. But in spite of their hardships, the Helmites remained a pious folk and never ceased to worship God. When the nights were bright and the moon was new, they stood outdoors beneath the open sky, and with faces upturned, chanted the traditional blessings.

Gimpel prayed along with them, but as befits the leading citizen of Helm, his mind was occupied with the more pressing earthly problems.

"What will happen to Helm?" he brooded. "Things are getting worse and worse. I must think of something soon." Rocking in prayer as pious Jews do, he gazed up at the bright moon. Suddenly, like a thunderbolt, he sprang up joyfully.

"Helmites, we are saved!" he cried.

Caught at the end of their prayers, the astonished

Helmites froze with the last words on the tips of their tongues.

"Helmites, give heed! We will capture the **moon!**" roared Gimpel.

"Capture the moon?" they repeated in utter **amaze**ment.

"Yes! You know that all good Jews must pray to the new moon each month. So here's what we'll do. We'll take down the moon, wrap it up carefully and hide it in our Synagogue. Then all the Jews from all over the world will have to come to us to pray to the moon. And by charging them all a small fee—nothing excessive, of course—we'll become the richest town in the world. All our problems will be solved."

"Helmites, we have a wizard amongst us. Sometimes we forget how much we owe him!" they cried to one another.

"Yes, we'll roll in riches," cried some others, "but don't forget, we'll give poor folks a piece of the moon for nothing."

"Wait," added Gimpel, "I haven't finished. I have more ideas. After we've kidnapped the moon, we'll wash it and scrub it and clean off its stains so that it will shine brighter and clearer. Then we'll comb it and polish it and rent it

out to all the big cities, and instead of using lanterns to light their streets at night, they can put up one bright, neat, well-washed moon. That'll save them lots of money and we'll amass a fortune."

"We are saved," chorused the Helmites, and they praised the Lord for having blessed them with Gimpel and his wisdom.

Suddenly, a small voice was heard. "I don't like to make a pest of myself," it said, "but would you mind telling me how we're going to get hold of the moon?" Everyone looked in the direction of the voice and there, sure enough, shaking with fright at his own boldness stood Berel the Beadle.

"How would *you* do it, Berel?" said Gimpel mockingly.

Berel was silent for a moment, then he offered timidly, "Well, we could collect all the ladders in Helm, tie them together, lean this great, long ladder against the Synagogue and—" to appease them, he added, "let me scramble up to lift the moon out of the sky."

"Just as I thought, the village fool has spoken," decreed Gimpel, whereupon all the Helmites took this as a signal to laugh uproariously. "Come tomorrow night and you'll see how it *will* be done," Gimpel concluded.

Poor Berel said to himself, "Why did I have to open my big mouth?"

The next evening, the market place was black with people. Not a Helmite was missing, and even the Rabbi was there, all wondering how Gimpel was going to perform the miracle. In the sky the moon shone brightly.

They had not long to wait. Gimpel soon arrived, followed by two Helmites carrying a tubful of red beet soup. After them came two more Helmites carrying a sack, a rope, and some sealing wax.

Halting in the center of the square, Gimpel commanded:

"Put the tub of red borsht here!"

The two Helmites obeyed.

Gimpel raised his voice so that all could hear:

"Helmites, lift up your eyes and behold! High above the moon is shining in the dark blue sky. Now look down into the tub of beet soup."

Thereupon the twelve foremost citizens approached and looked into the tub of red borsht.

"Aye," they said, and nodded their heads. "The same moon that is in the sky is here in the borsht."

"Hand me the sack and the rope and the sealing wax!" Gimpel thundered. The others hastened to do his bidding.

Quickly Gimpel covered the tub with the sack, tied the sack tightly with the rope, made ten knots and sealed each knot with wax.

"Now," said Gimpel triumphantly, "the moon is ours! We'll hide it in the Synagogue. And on the first dark night, when there is no moon in the sky, we'll be the masters!"

A couple of weeks passed. One dark night towards the end of the month, Gimpel announced:

"Helmites, this is the night we take out the moon."

Whereupon, twelve foremost citizens were given the honor of bringing the tub from the Synagogue to the square. There, Gimpel and the Mayor examined the treasure together and made sure that no one had tampered with it—the cords were knotted and the seals were untouched.

All around were assembled the people of Helm. Everyone wanted to see the moon taken out of the tub. They planned to carry it to the well, rinse it carefully in the clear water, and then hang it up again in the sky.

Gimpel went to work. He broke the wax seals and with a sharp knife, cut the knots. The ropes fell away. Quickly he snatched the sack off the tub and shouted:

"Let there be light! Let there be light!"

The people opened their mouths, all ready to shout with joy—but the night remained pitch black.

Gimpel thought that the moon must have gotten stuck on a nail. He overturned the tub of red borsht. It flowed all over the square, but the night still remained dark and black. Only the sweet smell of beet soup hung over the disappointed multitude.

In the silence, from way at the back of the crowd, someone was heard to mutter, "I'll bet *my* way would have worked." However, since Gimpel had failed to bring forth the moon, it was too dark to recognize Berel the Beadle.

It took a great deal of Gimpel's eloquence to explain to the Helmites that due to their negligence in failing to use preservatives, the moon had melted in the beet soup. For hours thereafter and late into the night, one could notice numbers of Helmites wandering around the square, peering at the cobblestones and actually seeing spots of light from bits of melted moon.

There was another little incident which occurred a few weeks later in connection with the moon event which shouldn't be left untold. One night Berel happened to run into Gimpel coming home from the Synagogue. Berel

pointed to the orange moon riding low in the heavens and righteously remarked, "I don't like to criticize you, brother Gimpel, but was it right telling us the moon melted when it really escaped?"

42

Gimpel replied with the greatest tolerance, "This is *not* the same moon as the one we captured, brother Beadle. Every month there is a new moon."

There's always a left and a right

IT WAS SHORTLY AFTER THE GREAT MOON DIS-aster. The Helmites were desperate—they could stand their poverty no longer. They crowded the square, calling for bread. Now the younger and bolder ones cried out against Gimpel, demanding that he sell the mill and bring prosperity back to Helm.

And for once, Gimpel, wisest man in Helm, didn't have an idea in his head. He stood in the Town Hall and listened to their cries and couldn't think of a thing. "Maybe it's because my stomach is empty too," he worriedly remarked to himself. Then it was that he called the young men to him and said at last:

"Fetch the miller! Let us sell him the mill!"

The neighboring miller came quickly, counted out his gold, and the mill was his. In no time at all, he had turned it into a windmill, and all was well in Helm again.

Once more, herring appeared on the Helmite's table instead of in his dreams. The menfolk worked in the fields, the women gossiped in the marketplace, the children played when they didn't fight and the old folks

argued whether it would rain today or tomorrow. All was well in Helm again.

Only the Rabbi wasn't satisfied. One fine Sabbath when the Synagogue was packed with people, he announced that a Town Meeting would be held that night. Immediately after evening services, the Helmites gathered to hear what the Rabbi had to say.

"Citizens of Helm!" he began. "God has blessed us and life is good. There is plenty of bread and even herring. We really want for nothing, but I tell you, something is wrong." A puzzled clamor arose, whereupon the Rabbi continued:

"Helmites, we must build a new Synagogue."

"What's wrong with the old one?" came the cry.

"The roof leaks, the walls are cracked and the paint is peeling," replied the Rabbi quickly.

"Then why not repair it?" asked a Helmite.

"What do you think we are," retorted the Rabbi, "paupers from Pultusk?"

"The Rabbi's right!" shouted the Helmites. "Helm must have a new Synagogue!"

At the break of dawn the very next day the Helmites met in the forest on the mountaintop. There they set to

work chopping down trees for their new Synogogue. Seizing saws and axes they fell upon the tall pines and the great oaks and soon sparks were flying all over the place. Tree after tree was felled by the industrious Helmites and within no time at all almost the entire forest had been turned into logs, stripped clean—trimmed of branches, peeled of bark and ready to be carried down the mountain.

Laboriously, with much grunting and more groaning, the Helmites carried the logs down into the valley, twelve men for each of the smaller logs and twenty men for the larger ones. Finally only one great oak log was left, so huge they could not budge it from the spot though they used as many men as could squeeze together along the length of it. It was such a beautiful log, however, they wouldn't think of abandoning it and so they sat there trying to figure out what to do.

They sat and sat and sat until along came Berel the Beadle who was running an errand for the Rabbi. When he learned of their plight, he thought for a while, scratched the back of his head and then suggested, "The log is round, isn't it? Round objects are rolled downhill, not carried. Don't you remember how you rolled me down the hill in the millstone? Why not roll it down?"

Though they had little respect for Berel's wisdom, they

remembered that what he said was true. In fact, they were even a little shocked that they hadn't thought of it themselves—they should have remembered how the millstones rolled down the hill, especially the one with Berel sticking out of it. True, round objects must be rolled downhill, not carried.

Whereupon the Helmites trudged down into the valley, painfully dragged all the logs back up the mountain one by one, and then carefully rolled them down again. Not forgetting the great, thick heavy log of oak, too—not the Helmites.

When Gimpel, who was supervising the building of the Synagogue, as he supervised everything in Helm, heard that all the logs were down in the valley, he went out to see how the work was getting on. What was his amazement to find the Helmites standing about in little groups, bickering, quarreling and doing nothing.

"Helmites, is this how you do God's work? Is this the way to build a Synagogue—with your tongues?" demanded Gimpel.

"Well," mumbled one of the Helmites, "we were about to carry the logs into the courtyard of the new Synagogue but we found out that each log has two ends, a left end and a right end."

"Well, and what's wrong with that?" asked Gimpel. "That's how it is with logs—they always have left and right ends."

"We know that," replied the Helmite, "but what's bothering us is who should go in first. Those carrying the right end say that *they* should be the ones to go in first, yet those carrying the left insist that *they* should."

"Excellent arguments," observed Gimpel. "They must be pondered."

So he pondered for a while. Took a pinch of snuff. Sneezed. And even coughed for good measure. Then his eyes brightened and his head cleared.

"I know what! Cut off the right end of the log, then only the left end will remain."

Satisfied, two Helmites sawed off the right end of a log and threw it away. Then six men on one side and six men on the other seized the log and began carrying it into the courtyard. They reached the entrance when, lo and behold, they noticed that the log still had two ends, a right and a left. Again the same problem—which end should go in first?

The Helmites dropped the log, returned to Gimpel and said:

"The log still has two ends and we still can't decide who should go in first."

Declared Gimpel:

"If the right-enders are so stubborn, then slice off the left end and let's have done with it. No more rights and no more lefts."

And so it was done. But, whether you believe it or not, the log still persisted in having two ends. No matter how much they cut off from one side or the other, there still remained a left and a right. By now Gimpel lost patience and commanded sternly:

"Carry the logs sideways—and let no one, either right or left, complain."

The Helmites lifted the logs and began carrying them sideways, but now a new problem arose—the street was too narrow.

Said Gimpel, "Now this concerns everybody. Let us call a Town Meeting."

And the wisest men in all Helm sat for seven nights and seven days and thought. When so many sages think for so long, they should think up something really clever. On the eighth day they issued the following proclamation:

"It has come to our attention that no matter how much one cuts a log, it still has two ends—a left and a right—

therefore the logs must be carried sideways. It has also come to our attention that the street is too narrow. Let us, then, tear down the houses on both sides of the street as far as the Synagogue."

And that is what the Helmites did. They tore down the houses on both sides of the street. Then, without further ado, they carried the logs sideways right into the courtyard of the new Synagogue.

The Helmites set to work building their new Synagogue. They worked with zeal, and in no time at all, the walls were up and there was the roof, its bright red shingles proudly gleaming in the sun. So far, so good. No quarrels, not even a cross word. That is, sad to relate, until it came to laying the floor. Then the fur began to fly. Helm was split in two, those in favor of smooth boards and those against. Never was there such a commotion in Helm!

And what was it all about? Nothing trivial, I assure you, for after all, this was Helm and not Shedlitz or some other town full of simpletons. As everyone knows, on that most solemn fast day known as Yom Kippur, Jews remove their shoes in the Synagogue and pray in their stockinged feet. Now if the floor boards were not planed smooth, some Helmite might get a splinter in his foot, a splinter leads to

a sore foot, a sore foot makes one limp, limping often causes one to fall and break your neck, and reader, do you want a broken neck?

The opposition in Helm argued in this fashion: true, there is some danger if the boards are not planed, but there is even greater peril if the floor is too smooth. For on Simchas Torah, which is a very joyous holiday, Jews dance about the Synagogue with the Holy Torah in their arms. On a planed floor, they'd naturally slip and fall. Then all of Helm would have to fast and mourn for forty days and forty nights because the Holy Torah had been dropped.

Gimpel carefully weighed the arguments, decided that both sides were right, and rendered the following solution which was not without true Helmite wisdom:

"The boards must indeed be smooth because the danger of splinters on Yom Kippur is great, but let only one side be planed, then lay the smooth, planed side face downwards with the rough side up so that when the Helmites dance on Simchas Torah they won't slip and fall with the Holy Torah in their arms."

And so it was done. The new Synagogue was completed and Helm celebrated. One and all, they came for the festivities. They danced and sang, ate and drank, and made

merry all through the night. Only one person was sad, that was Mottel the Mayor.

Berel the Beadle noticed him looking gloomily at their handsome new Synagogue and couldn't understand it. "What's the matter, Mayor Mottel, why the long face?" he inquired.

"The Synagogue is too beautiful," muttered the Mayor.

"Too beautiful?" exclaimed Berel in amazement. "You remind me of the bridegroom who complained that his bride was too pretty."

"Listen to the fool," retorted Mottel. "Didn't it ever occur to you that it's so beautiful it might be stolen?"

"Of course," interrupted Gimpel, who had overheard the conversation. "The Mayor is right. The danger is very serious. Tomorrow morning, Berel, before anything else, take a brush and paint '*Zeh Hashul Shaich Lechelem*' in huge letters on the front wall of the Synagogue. That means 'This Synagogue belongs to Helm.'"

Mottel was overjoyed. "Now that's an idea! Let them steal it. What can they do with it? Wherever they take it, everyone will know that it's stolen goods."

One fine morning, some weeks after Berel had carefully painted the inscription on the Synagogue, what was his

surprise to discover that it was not the Synagogue that had been stolen but the money in the alms-box. All the leading citizens of Helm were excited. The box had been securely fastened to the wall with twelve long nails, but the thieves had not been lazy and had made short work of it. A Town Meeting was called to discuss what was to be done now. Nail up a new box? Thieves would steal it again. Not nail up any box at all? What kind of a Synagogue would it be without an alms-box?

Suggested Mottel: "Hang the box high in the air on a chain fastened to the highest rafter in the ceiling and the thieves will not be able to get at it."

But Berel pointed out the weakness of the mayor's proposal. "True, hanging it high in the air is an excellent idea.

The thieves will not be able to get at it—but neither will we. Then what good is an alms-box that you can't throw alms into?"

"Well, can *you* think of anything better?" Berel was asked. Berel couldn't. So again Gimpel had to come to the rescue. Of course, it took him seven days and seven nights. Then he said: "True, we *should* hang the alms-box high in the air where thieves can't get at it. But we should also have a ladder reaching to the alms-box for those who wish to throw a little something into it. In addition, the ladder should have the following warning in big, red letters: 'This ladder is only for those who wish to drop alms into the alms-box. It is against the law for thieves to use it.'"

Help, thieves in Helm!

SOME YEARS PASSED. THINGS WERE GOING WELL **55** in Helm. The crops were plentiful and all through the town the bins were bursting with grain. Hitherto, there had never been enough of anything and suddenly now there was too much of everything. The Helmites were worried. They'd never had this kind of a problem before. Something had to be done. They called a Town Meeting.

For seven days and seven nights they thrashed the matter around but here was something unusual that baffled even the leading citizens of Helm. Even Gimpel. It was finally decided that this was a question of philosophical proportions and so they called upon their philosopher, Pinya.

Pinya pondered and pondered. He took off his shoes and pondered some more. In vain. Pinya had to admit that he too was stumped. But he did have one idea.

"Whereas Helm never suffered from prosperity before the miller came to our town and whereas we do so suffer now, therefore let it be concluded that we demand an explanation from the miller," he sagely pronounced. The

Helmites sighed with relief and thereupon Berel the Beadle was dispatched to summon the miller.

When the situation was explained to the miller, he promptly offered a suggestion.

"Helmites," he said, "why don't you go into business?"

The Helmites looked in perplexity at one another.

"What does it mean, this going into business, O miller?"

"Going into business," explained the miller, "means buying and selling."

The Helmites burst into laughter.

"Listen to him! If we buy something, naturally we need it for ourselves, so why should we sell it?"

The miller was especially patient because he knew he was dealing with Helmites:

"Buy things you do not need and—"

The Helmites nearly split their sides laughing. Without letting him finish, they shouted:

"Why should we buy things we don't need? Are you crazy? Are you from Shedlitz?"

The patient miller tried again:

"Buy things you yourselves don't need and sell them to the farmers who pass through Helm."

Realizing that the miller was serious, the Helmites inquired further:

"How does it work?"

"Well, the idea is to buy cheap and sell dear. For example, you buy a pair of boots for five guldens and sell it for six guldens."

Marvelled the Helmites:

"Really? One gets a gulden for nothing? One neither sows nor plows nor does anything, and one gets a gulden? Why?"

"That's the way business is done."

"If that's all there is to business, maybe we ought to try it," agreed the Helmites.

So Helm took to trading. Many sold their fields and orchards, their cows and their chickens and their sheep. With the money, they built shops and filled them with all sorts of good things—bundles of flax, kerosene for the lamps, aprons for the women, meal, salt, yeast, white eggs and brown eggs, boots for every kind of foot, nails, axes, scythes, beads for the young girls, and even a little vodka for when the heart needed warming.

Soon the farmers in the neighboring villages heard of the wonderful wares in the new shops of Helm, so they flocked to the town at harvest time to grind their grain and buy what they needed. Everybody was pleased, the miller was pleased, the neighboring farmers were pleased, and

the Helmites were especially pleased for business **was** good.

58 But suddenly all Helm shook to its very foundations. A blacksmith had come to town. He settled in the center of Helm's bustling market-place and was quickly loaded down with work. It was his very first day in town. Dusk was beginning to fall. The good folk of Helm had closed their shops for the night and were wending their way towards the Synagogue for evening prayers when they passed the strange, new smithy. There they caught sight of the blacksmith at his forge. With huge hammer in hand, he was beating a glowing piece of red-hot iron and his face was shiny and black as coal. The Helmites stood still, frozen with horror. The smith was black and gypsies are black. What does that prove? Of course, that the smith was a gypsy! And the proverb says that all gypsies are thieves! Indeed, things looked bad for Helm! The swarthy blacksmith who was a thief would soon walk off with everything. They would be robbed of all their riches. Not a spool of thread would be left in Helm.

So they called a Town Meeting.

For seven days and seven nights the Helmites sat and talked. They talked until they talked the whole matter

through. When do thieves do their thieving? At night. Then the calamity could easily be prevented. The shop-keepers would sleep by day and watch the shops by night. A worthy plan.

And that was exactly what the Helmites did. The shop-keepers slept by day and kept the shops open at night. But soon they came to realize that this would not do. At night nobody came to the shops to buy, and by day, when the farmers did come to town, the shops were closed.

Then what's to be done? After all, there was no choice but to keep the shops open by day. The shopkeepers would have to go back to sleeping at night. Ah, but who would guard the shops? Simple—a night watchman. The watch-man would sleep by day and watch by night. And so said, so done.

Again there was peace and quiet. But soon the summer passed, and cold winds began to blow. The night watch-man complained to the shopkeepers that the nights were raw and windy and he was afraid he'd catch cold.

When they heard this, the shopkeepers became terribly alarmed. This was no trifling matter! The watchman would catch cold! A calamitous thing! A cold leads to pneumonia, and pneumonia might kill a man before you can say *Berel the Beadle*. That was all the merchants

needed! If the watchman died, a widow and seven orphans would have to be cared for. A new watchman would have to be hired. The town would be impoverished.

What's to be done? Came the suggestion: Let a sheepskin coat be bought for the watchman. In a sheepskin coat he would be warm and comfortable on the coldest of nights and so would never catch cold. But Gimpel, the foremost citizen of Helm, objected:

"I wear a sheepskin coat. Now, if the watchman also wears a sheepskin coat, how will the town know who is Gimpel and who is the watchman?"

A just grievance.

So the Helmites pondered further. They sat for another seven days and nights and could not think their way through. On the last day Tevya the Tailor arose and said:

"I have a plan. Here in Helm we make sheepskin coats in the correct manner—with the fur on the inside, so that it keeps the body warm. In America, which is on the other side of the world, they wear fur coats backwards, with the fur on the outside. Let's make the night-watchman an inside-out coat, with the fur on the outside. Then everyone will know who is Gimpel and who is the night-watchman."

Gimpel was satisfied, but suddenly the night-watchman

began protesting fearfully, "What do you want to do—murder me in cold blood? It's a trap! If I put on a coat like that," he shouted, "a wolf might take me for a sheep. And you know what a wolf does to a sheep!"

The Helmites sat as though transfixed, quivering with fright. All they needed now was to have their watchman gobbled up by a wolf. Seven orphans and a widow!

But Tevya the Tailor had a real Helmite head on his shoulders. He stroked his beard and said:

"Get a horse and put the watchman on it. Then the wolf will see that the watchman isn't a real sheep. Whoever heard of a sheep riding on a horse?"

And that was what they did. Tevya made an inside-out coat for the watchman. Helm bought a horse for the watchman, and the watchman, wearing an inside-out fur coat, sat on the horse and guarded the shops.

But a few days later the watchman came back with a new complaint.

"What's wrong now?" asked the anxious Helmites.

"Last night the horse decided to go wandering," related the trembling watchman. "He galloped out of the town and carried me as far as the deep clay pits. After all, he might have fallen into one of them and I might have been killed!"

The quaking Helmites called another Town Meeting. They talked and thought, thought and talked, and neither thought nor talked their way to anything worthwhile. Gimpel took a pinch of snuff, sneezed, and stated:

"Since this deals with a horse, let's ask a teamster."

So they called a teamster and told him the whole story. Being a Helmite teamster, he had a true Helmite solution:

"Aye, let the watchman sit on the horse but since the horse might decide to run away with the watchman and dump him, sheepskin coat and all, into the deep pits, therefore let the horse be tied to a post."

Surely this was good, prudent advice, but now a new problem arose. Each shopkeeper wanted the post to be placed near his shop.

They quarreled and complained and could not find a solution until late in the night. At last they arrived at a compromise: they would place the post near the Town Hall since that belonged to everybody.

So they did just that. Again everyone was satisfied, and again the town was peaceful and quiet.

But what must be, must be. At dawn, one fine, frosty morning the watchman knocked politely on the shutters of the houses, as he did every morning. "Time to awake,

Helmites," he called, "but you'd better hurry," he added, "thieves have emptied your shops."

Out of their beds flew the Helmite shopkeepers, more dead than alive. Without even bothering to dress, they dashed to their shops, and when they saw that the doors had been broken open, the shelves emptied, and not a shoe-lace nor a spool of thread left by the thieves, there arose

a wailing and lamenting. The dismayed shopkeepers dragged the watchman to the Rabbi. The whole town followed excitedly.

"Rabbi, the watchman has failed us. Here we pay him good money to watch our stores and he lets thieves rob us of everything we possessed."

Asked the Rabbi:

"What kind of a watchman are you if you let thieves rob Helm?"

Replied the watchman:

"Rabbi, I admit I saw the thieves break the locks. With my own eyes, I watched them carrying the wares out of the shops. But I could do nothing. I was sitting on the horse and the horse was tied firmly to the post near the Town Hall, which, as you know, is some distance from the shops. Now, I ask you, Rabbi, can a cat walk on water or a man fly through the air?"

The Rabbi stroked his beard and said: "True, but why didn't you untie the horse, gallop over to the shops and catch the thieves?"

Replied the watchman:

"Rabbi, that was just what I wanted to do, but I reminded myself that the horse might take it into its head to gallop away with me and dump me right into the deep

clay pits. So being frightened that I'd be killed, my children orphaned and my wife widowed, how could I have untied the horse, I ask you?"

The Rabbi rejoined:

"True, you shouldn't risk orphaning your children and widowing your wife, but why didn't you get off the horse, dash over to the shops and catch the thieves?"

Replied the watchman:

"But, Rabbi, you forget I'm still wearing my American inside-out coat and I was afraid a wolf would mistake me for a sheep and gobble me up."

Said the Rabbi:

"That is a good reason for not getting off the horse, but you still should have thrown off your fur coat, run to the shops and caught the thieves."

Replied the watchman with tears in his eyes:

"But, Rabbi, the night was cold and frosty. I was afraid I would catch cold. A cold leads to pneumonia and pneumonia would be the end of me. Seven little orphans would remain after me, Rabbi, and a widow too!"

"Yes," replied the Rabbi gently, "it is correct for a father of seven children to guard his health. But you are still not right. You could have begun shouting: 'Help, Helmites, awake! Thieves are looting the shops!'"

The watchman looked at the Rabbi in surprise and said:

"Rabbi, I don't understand you! If I had shouted 'Help!' I would have awakened the shopkeepers before it was time. Now, Rabbi, with all due respect to you, if I awaken the shopkeepers at night, I am not doing my job properly. The shopkeepers hired me for just this purpose —that I should be awake all night so that they could sleep. If I had cried for help I would have awakened them and they would have been angry."

The Rabbi took a pinch of snuff and said:

"You are right after all. You are a good, faithful watchman. You did your work honorably, as you were told."

And what do you suppose?

The Helmites gave their good, faithful night watchman an increase in wages.

How the Helmites bought a barrel of justice

THUS BUSINESS CAME TO HELM, THIEVES AND all. And with it, the rich got richer and the poor got worries. And as always happens, the poor came to be jealous of the rich and the rich came to fear the poor. That was the way of the world and even Helm was no exception.

In the days when Helmites were building watermills on mountaintops, before they went into business, the people were neither rich nor poor. But now there were those who lived in fine brick houses and clothed themselves in expensive garments made of rare cloths. Even their little children wore raiment of the best wool interwoven with silk thread and trimmed with velvet.

They fared on the finest foods, on raisin-studded *chaleh* and honey tarts yellow as saffron, stuffed young hens and roast duck dripping with gravy. When it came to this, the rich in Helm were no different from the rich all over the world.

And the same with the poor. They suffered and struggled as the poor do everywhere. If once in seven years, a poor Helmite could buy a scrap of clothing for himself, what would it be made of but cotton? The women made their own dresses of cheap calico and gingham while the children never saw anything but made-overs from father's overcoat and hand-me-downs from big sister's petticoats.

The poor had to be content with potatoes flavored with herring water to fill their stomachs. Once in a great while they would allow themselves the luxury of buying the feet and heads of hens that had been ordered by the rich.

Even in the Synagogue, the well-to-do would be seated in their own pews at the East Wall near the Holy Ark while the poor would stand squeezed together behind the pulpit, near the stove and alongside the wash basin. But the poor were so many in Helm that they jammed the little space allowed them, leaving no room for benches to rest on when they became weary.

Finally, one hot summer Sabbath when the heat had become unbearable and the crush and stuffiness behind the pulpit could no longer be endured, the long-suffering poor stopped the services and appealed to the Rabbi:

"We claim our ancient right to interrupt the services and to prevent the Torah Reading until our wrongs are righted."

"What are your wrongs, my people?" asked the Rabbi gently.

"Rabbi, why do the rich live on milk and honey while we live on air?" cried a cobbler lad.

And before the Rabbi could answer came another cry from a tailor's apprentice:

"Why do the rich wear silks and stuff themselves with choice meats while we go around in cotton rags and begrudge ourselves even a little lung and soup cooked from bones?"

Then came a thunderous shout from the midst of the crowd, "O Rabbi, there is no justice in Helm!"

Now all the throng took up the cry, "There is no justice in Helm!"

The Rabbi took a pinch of snuff, sneezed twice, then once more for good measure and thought for seven days and seven nights, for this was the weightiest problem that had ever been set before him. Then slowly and with great deliberation came his reply:

"True, there is no justice in Helm. But it must be somewheres since the Holy Torah guarantees it. It must have slipped away to some other place while we were busy doing business. Therefore let us send two messengers out into the world to buy some justice and bring it back to Helm—enough for rich and poor alike."

And so the two messengers set out on their journey into

the world to buy some justice. Wherever they went, they would ask:

"Good people, can you tell us where to buy a little justice?"

Everywhere they were given the same reply:

"No use looking. We too lack that little item. If we knew where to get some, we'd sell the shirts off our backs."

The Helmites rode on. They rode and rode until they came to Warsaw.

They walked through the crowded streets of the city and saw great markets with fancy shop windows, stores crammed with all kinds of wares, but not a sign of justice anywhere.

They walked on, continuing their search, until they came to an immense store which was bigger than all the stores in Helm put together. The two Helmites gazed open-mouthed at the wonderful displays in the shop windows and one said to the other:

"In such a great trading house, where there are so many different kinds of merchandise, there must be at least a little bit of justice around, even if it's been stuck away on a back shelf somewheres."

A pair of Warsaw rogues caught sight of the two coun-

try yokels staring into the window. Being on the lookout for some easy money and sensing that here was likely prey, the clever rascals went up to the Helmites and said:

"Friends, how would you like to get a good bargain? We can sell you the Vistula Bridge cheap, or if you can't use the Bridge we can sell you the Saxony Gardens. Or perhaps you're interested in the Warsaw Synagogue? We can sell you anything your heart desires."

Replied the Helmites:

"No, good folks, we don't want to buy the Vistula Bridge or the Saxony Gardens. And why would we need the Warsaw Synagogue when we have a fine, new Synagogue of our own in Helm?"

"O, so you're Helmites?" exclaimed the scoundrels, as their greedy eyes began to gleam.

"Aye, we're Helmites," replied the two messengers, pleased with the new respect the men seemed to show them.

"And what is it that such two wise men from Helm seek in Warsaw?" politely asked the rogues.

"Justice is what we seek," responded the Helmites. "We have travelled far and wide and cannot find a crumb of justice to save our lives."

Replied the others:

"Look no further, Helmites, your search is ended. We'll sell you as much justice as you want."

The messengers from Helm rejoiced and asked eagerly: "Can you sell us a whole barrelful?"

"Well," said the others with feigned hesitation, "justice, as you know, is an expensive article. But if you can afford it, we'll manage to get you a barrelful."

The Helmites were in seventh heaven:

"Will two thousand gold pieces be enough?"

"Is that all you have?" asked the Warsaw thieves, trying to conceal their glee.

"That's every kopek," replied the Helmites.

"Then it will have to do. After all, we can't let you go back to Helm without justice," said the swindlers. "Come with us."

A few hours later, the knaves delivered a full barrel of justice, nailed tight and sealed all around, to the messengers from Helm who almost fell over themselves with excitement as they handed over the two thousand gold pieces. At last their quest was ended!

Before the rogues departed, they warned the Helmites:

"Make sure not to jostle the barrel on the way. The cover might fly off and some of the treasure might be

spilled. You know how hard it is to get justice these days."

"You don't have to tell us that," replied the Helmites. "Why, we'll carry it as though it were a steaming bowl of delicious chicken soup."

The Helmites thanked their benefactors, said good-bye and parted.

There was great rejoicing in Helm. The messengers had just returned with a whole barrelful of justice. Imagine! A whole barrelful! Now all would be well in Helm again with justice enough for rich and poor.

After elaborate ceremonies in the town square, to Mottel

the Mayor went the honor of opening the precious barrel. With bated breath he broke the seals, loosened the nails and pried open the cover while all of Helm crowded around, eager to see what the justice of the world looked like.

As the cover was reverently lifted, what was their amazement when an odor assailed their nostrils—the foul odor of rotten fish. Springing back in horror, Mottel cried:

"Alas, the justice is spoiled!"

Then Gimpel too stuck his nose into the barrel, took one whiff and jumped back, crying dismally:

"Aye, the justice of the world smells bad!"

And now a moaning and a wailing arose over the square as the grief-stricken Helmites repeated to one another: "Alas, the justice is spoiled! The justice of the world smells bad! Woe is us! What shall we do?"

Whereupon Gimpel, richest man in Helm, exclaimed, "Take heed, O ye Helmites who complain of the justice in Helm." And pointing pompously to the barrel, he bellowed, "That's the kind of justice you have in the rest of the world!"

The throng stood there, bewildered, but the young cobbler lad sprang up to answer Gimpel: "Poor people of Helm, listen to me, if there is no justice in Helm, and even

the justice of the world has been spoiled, then it doesn't matter what we do. We can do whatever we want."

The tailor's apprentice took up the cry. "The rich are few, we are many. No one can stop us."

"Let's break into the shops," then shouted the cobbler lad, "and take whatever we need."

"Aye, aye!" clamored the poor people of Helm excitedly. "We'll take the finest cloths," someone cried. "And the choicest meats for the Sabbath!" from another. "And in the Synagogue let's take the pews by the East Wall. Let the rich stand behind the pulpit near the stove and alongside the wash basin."

Hearing the tumult, the rich became alarmed. They called a Town Meeting immediately, and invited the cobbler lad to sit at the right of the Mayor and the tailor's apprentice at his left, in the places of honor. There was talking and thinking and thinking and talking for seven days and seven nights, and at last they came to a brilliant compromise:

"From this day on whenever an ox is slaughtered, let the entire animal consist only of the choicest parts, such as breast and flank. Let all parts be alike. Then there will be no difference which part one buys.

"Likewise, let it be known to all that the entire Syna-

gogue is the East Wall and center pews. Then, to be sure, there will be no difference where a person sits.

"Likewise, let there be no distinction between satin and gingham, silk and cotton. Let all stuffs be alike. Then it will make no difference what sort of clothes one wears.

"But since it happens that the rich may be foolish enough to wish to pay more in order to sit nowhere else but at the *former* East Wall; likewise, since they may desire to pay more for the *former* breast and flank meats, and for *former* silks and velvets and wools—then let them be welcome to their foolishness."

And so it was done. All was peaceful again in Helm. Both the rich and the poor were content. As for the rich, everything was as of old. Yet for the poor, times had changed. They would go about, saying:

"Helm has certainly improved. The entire Synagogue now is East Wall and center pews. The whole ox is breast and flank meat. All cloths are satin, silk and wool. We poor live on the fat of the land. Gone are the old, unhappy days when the rich lived on milk and honey and we lived on air. Now, all are equal!"

Ayè, it was peaceful again in Helm. Times had changed —and everything was as of old.

OUR OLD FRIEND GIMPEL WAS NOW A man of great wealth. His was the finest shop, he owned the largest house, he wore the best sheepskin coat and naturally he was president of the Synagogue.

The Lord had also blessed Gimpel with an only son named Yossel who was the apple of his father's eye. When Gimpel deemed it time for the boy to be married, he set forth in search of a bride befitting his darling Yossel—a bride beyond compare. All Helm must ring with her praises.

Gimpel sought long and hard and at last his quest was rewarded. In the great city of Warsaw, he found a beautiful maiden, daughter of the most pious Jew in the realm. She was as accomplished as she was beautiful; she could play the piano and speak with the greatest elegance. She never said "Thank you," as is the custom in Helm, but "Merci," as the Frenchmen say. When she ate, she chewed

delicately with her little front teeth like a real princess, and on her head, she wore a tiny bonnet with a tall blue feather. It was whispered about that the bonnet had been sent from Paris especially for her. She carried a red silk parasol and wore pink satin slippers with high heels. Besides all this, she was truly pious and could read her prayers as fast as the Rabbi.

Hiring the most elaborate carriage in Warsaw, Gimpel brought the beautiful maid to Helm. When the townsfolk saw her promenading through the market-place, so fair and so noble, they said to one another:

"Gimpel has truly found a princess for his Yossel."

All Helm envied Gimpel as he puffed and crowed over the match. And he promised to hold a wedding the likes of which had never been seen before. There would be musicians from Plotzk, waiters from Warsaw, a cook from Odessa, a Cantor from Vilna and a *badchon* * from Brod. There would also be mountains of honey cake, barrels of *schnapps,* and as far as the wedding soup was concerned—it is known as the *Golden Broth*—ah, that would be a treat fit for the angels.

A Helmite keeps his word.

Gimpel ordered musicians from Plotzk, waiters from

* An entertainer, an improvising rhymster.

Warsaw, a cook from Odessa, a Cantor from Vilna, and a *badchon* from Brod. To buy the fowl for the Golden Broth, he travelled to the distant city of Dorpetz, beyond Koenigsburg—to Dorpetz, famous for its plump white hens, its well-fed ducks and its fatted geese.

In went Gimpel to the finest butcher in the city and said pompously:

"Butcher of Dorpetz, I want the best, the plumpest hens and ducks and geese that you have. Money is no object. I'm Gimpel of Helm and my son Yossel is going to be married."

Said the butcher:

"Certainly, Gimpel, great merchant of Helm. I've heard of you. Don't worry. For you, I'll select the finest fowl in the city. O, not just ordinary hens and ducks and geese but each one better and tastier than the other, and all as rich and juicy as pure *schmaltz*!"

Now *schmaltz* is a most delicately flavored food, a fat that comes from the best kinds of fowl, and when Gimpel heard the butcher of Dorpetz compare his birds to *schmaltz*, the great and wise merchant from Helm became indignant. For is it not obvious that one always seeks to make a poorer thing seem better, a weaker thing, stronger? Does one not speak of the copper pan that shines like gold,

of the man who is strong as iron? So it must follow that the *schmaltz* was better than the fowl.

Said Gimpel:

"You can't fool me, butcher. No hens or ducks or geese for me. I'm a rich merchant and I can afford the best of everything, especially for my son's wedding. I shall use nothing but pure *schmaltz* for the Golden Broth."

The butcher could hardly believe his ears, so he asked: "What's this, are you crazy?"

By this time Gimpel was really angry.

"You mean to tell me you won't sell me any *schmaltz*? All right, I'll buy it somewhere else."

The butcher nearly burst into laughter but realizing that he was dealing with a Helmite, he caught himself in time and replied politely:

"Bless you, my good Gimpel, but what made you think that I don't want to sell you any *schmaltz*? You want *schmaltz*? Then *schmaltz* it'll be. Why, I'll sell you the very best *schmaltz* in all Poland, *schmaltz* as fragrant and yellow as olive oil from the far-off Holy Land."

When Gimpel heard *this,* he exclaimed furiously:

"Swindler of a butcher! Scoundrel of a trickster! Olive oil must be better then. Olive oil I can get in any grocery store. What do I need a rascal like you for?"

No sooner said than done. Leaving the butcher bewildered, Gimpel dashed out, ran into the largest grocery store on the square and said breathlessly:

"I am Gimpel, leading citizen of Helm! My one and only son is to be married, and for the Golden Broth at his wedding I want the finest olive oil that money can buy."

Reflected the astonished shopkeeper: "Listen to this—something new! Olive oil for the Golden Broth! Truly, this Gimpel must be a real Helmite from Helm! But who am I to teach him sense?" So, with a great show of courtesy, the shopkeeper replied:

"There in the corner stands a barrel of olive oil that is like one of the seven wonders of the world, olive oil as clear and pure and transparent as water fresh from the well."

At this, Gimpel nearly choked with amazement. "This means, then," he muttered to himself, "that well-water is better for the Golden Broth than olive oil, which is better than *schmaltz*, which is better than hens and ducks and geese. Then why did I have to drag myself all the way to Dorpetz when everyone knows that Helm has the best well-water in Europe?"

Without another word, Gimpel departed and took himself back to Helm. When he came home, he rolled up his

sleeves, hastened to the square and drew a bucketful of water from the town well. Carrying it home carefully so as not to spill a drop, he said to his Odessa cook:

"From this precious liquid you will cook the Golden Broth. Nothing so ordinary as hens, ducks or geese for us!"

Not being a Helmite, the cook looked startled, stared at the water, then at Gimpel, then back at the water again. Puzzled, she started to taste the water, when Gimpel shrieked:

"Stop, fool! What are you doing? That's for the Golden Broth!"

Whereupon the cook remembered that she was in Helm, shrugged her shoulders and said to herself: "Now there's a Helmite soup for you—made from well-water!" Aloud she mumbled:

"Mercy on us!" Then she quickly added, "Yes, of course, the Golden Broth at your son's wedding will certainly be something different."

The day before the wedding the whole town was bubbling like a teakettle over the fire. Before noon everyone drove out beyond the town gates to meet the kinsmen of the bride and escort them into Helm. Then the musicians

from Plotzk arrived. Now came the waiters from Warsaw in stovepipe hats and cutaways. Then followed the Vilna Cantor, and at last, the bride herself!

The musicians from Plotzk began to play and the Helmites started dancing and hopping in time to the music. The townsfolk drank one another's health in schnapps, wine and mead, and topped it off with honey cake. Truly, on that day there was merry-making in Helm, for the town's leading citizen was marrying off his only son to a refined and elegant lady. The air was laden with the fragrant smells of stuffed-fish, roasted meats and freshly baked twisted *chaleh*.

And now the wedding ceremony was about to begin. The bride was being led to the canopy. At the head of the procession went the musicians from Plotzk playing a new wedding march especially composed for the occasion. Following the Plotzk musicians came Berel with his fiddle and Shmerel with his big bass viol. They would show the Plotzkers that the Helmites could pluck a string or two. Then came the kinsfolk of the bride, attired in their finest garments. After them marched the towns people of Helm, one and all carrying lighted candles and burning torches.

The procession arrived at the courtyard of the Synagogue for in those days weddings were held outdoors under

the skies. The canopy was in its place and the bride came to a halt beneath it. All were silent as they waited for the Cantor to begin the first note of the Wedding Blessings. But what was their surprise to see him standing there with mouth open and no sound emerging. They looked around and lo and behold, there was not a sign of the bridegroom. In the commotion, they had forgotten all about him.

Cries of "Where is the groom? Where is the groom?" arose from all over, and then and there they realized that

he must have been left behind. But even in Helm, a bride cannot be married without a groom, so a frantic search was begun at once. They looked for him in his father's house, they looked for him in his uncle's house, they even looked for him at the shop where he always bought his favorite honey cake, but he was nowhere to be found. Alarmed, they rushed back to the Synagogue and cried out in amazement when they stumbled upon Yossel standing among the little boys, holding a lighted candle in his hand and gazing expectantly at the bride along with all the other Helmites.

He was hustled home and dressed in his wedding clothes. Over these was placed a white silk robe, over the robe a sable coat and on his head a seven-pointed headdress. Then he was led to the bridal canopy. At last the bride would have her groom.

The Cantor coughed delicately, as is customary with Cantors the world over, and was about to begin the Wedding Blessings when the Rabbi discovered that the bride and groom were facing west, and everybody knows that the law says a bride and groom must face east during the ceremony. Something had to be done at once.

The resourceful Gimpel suggested that the canopy under which the bridal pair was standing be turned

around. The Rabbi motioned to Berel the Beadle to turn the canopy. This was done and the Cantor was about to begin when it was again discovered that Yossel and his bride were still facing west. Once more Berel turned the bridal canopy, but it was no use. He turned the canopy this way, that way and every which way, but when all the fuss and to-do were over, the bride and groom were still facing west. A tumult arose from the assembled guests—the great Gimpel should have arranged everything in advance! How could he have been so careless?

Who knows, the couple might have been standing there to this very day if it had not been for Berel the Beadle who got the brilliant idea of turning the couple instead of the canopy. However, the best he could do was to get them facing south, for it was well known that Berel had difficulty distinguishing left from right. But finally the kinsfolk of the bride came to the rescue, took the couple by the shoulders and turned them to the east. It helped. The Cantor began the Wedding Blessings and the choir chimed in with great zest.

The ceremony proceeded slowly and everyone had a properly solemn face as he should have, even the sophisticated city folk from Warsaw. When at last it was over, the wedding throng relaxed into smiles and the musicians

struck up a happy tune. Gimpel's old mother Sossel who was a fine, stout woman pushed her brightly colored shawl behind her ears to show her glittering new earrings—a gift from her husband especially for the wedding—and taking a few skipping steps, called out loudly: "Bring me the twisted bridal *challehs*!"

Quickly they handed her the two glistening twists. Holding them aloft, one in each hand, she turned to face the bride and groom and began to dance. Everyone clapped hands in time with the music and forming a jolly procession with the portly Sossel skipping in the lead, they marched towards the hall where the wedding feast was already spread. But suddenly someone shrieked *Fire*! and there before the astonished eyes of the guests, the entire roof of the hall was soon enveloped in flames. Alas, 'ere one could say *Berel the Beadle*, the hall itself was burned

down to the very ground. And that was the sad, sad end of Gimpel's wedding feast.

Helm might soon have forgotten all about the fire were it not for that lost supper. It was talked about and worried about and worried about and talked about until finally a Town Meeting was called to determine the mysterious cause of the fire. Now, although they thought and thought and thought for seven days and seven nights, no one really ever found out what started it. Some said that it must have been those new-fangled things called cigarettes which had been smoked by some of the kinsfolk from Warsaw. Others insisted, no, while certainly it was true that the fire was the result of Warsaw carelessness, the actual cause was those peculiar little sticks which the city people used to light their cigarettes.

Then along came Berel with one of his ridiculous notions. He thought he'd noticed one little boy tossing away a burning candle just before starting to clap his hands. It might have alighted on the thatched roof of the hall, suggested Berel. But whatever it was, whether a new-fangled cigarette, a peculiar match or just a plain, ordinary candle, the wedding supper was gone forever and not a single soul was destined to taste Gimpel's Golden Broth made of crystal clear well-water.

All because of a pair of shoes

CONSTERNATION BROKE OUT ALL OVER Helm after the wedding fire. The townsfolk became terribly alarmed—they must guard against such a calamity happening again. But how? Matters like these cannot be decided while standing on one foot, so once again a Town Meeting was called.

The Helmites thought for seven days and seven nights but no one came forward with a plan. Everyone knew that fire is put out by water but in Helm water has to be drawn from the river and the river was too distant from the town. So far, not so good.

When Gimpel saw that his fellow townsfolk could not, as usual, solve the problem without his aid, he took a pinch of snuff, sneezed loudly, stroked his beard and said:

"Helmites, I have a plan."

"What is it? The plan, the plan! Tell us the plan!" came the eager shouts.

"Remember how cleverly the Jews of Warsaw turned Yossel and his bride around so that they faced the east?" asked Gimpel.

"Of course we do," came the reply. "What about it?"

"Well, if the Jews of Warsaw are so smart at weddings, maybe they're just as smart when it comes to fires. Let's send a messenger to Warsaw to find out how they put out fires."

The Helmites rejoiced at this, crying out, "O good and wise Gimpel, what would we do without you? Surely the Lord blessed us when he sent you amongst us."

Then the question arose, who should go to Warsaw? Naturally, the wisest man in Helm. And who could that be—not counting the matchless Gimpel, of course—but Pinya the Philosopher. Now, in a town as full of wise men as Helm, how did Pinya come to be known as the Philosopher? Herein lies a tale.

One day Pinya—who was not called the Philosopher then—came home, sat down on a stool in the centre of the room, propped his head on his right hand—and just sat there.

When his wife came in, she cried out in alarm, "Pinya, what are you doing?"

"Thinking," came back the sage reply.

"What are you thinking about?" asked his wife.

"How can I tell, foolish woman," retorted Pinya, "if

the thought is still hatching in my head. Let me be, will you?"

Pinya's anger frightened his wife so she let him be, sitting there on a stool in the middle of the room with his head propped on his right hand.

A day passed, then another day. Pinya neither ate nor drank but sat there, thinking.

Then his wife began pleading with him:

"Pinya, Pinya, you'll get sick. Have something to eat, for God's sake!"

He shook his head. For to Pinya, thinking was much more important than eating, sleeping and drinking put together, and he would not stop until he had thought his thought through to the end.

But his wife insisted:

"Pinya, Pinya, it is three days and three nights since you have eaten!"

Pinya, faint with hunger, replied in a thin, weak voice:

"Let me be, woman. Don't you see a thought is hatching in my head?"

Realizing that things were going badly and that her husband might think so long she would become a widow, God forbid, she went to see the Rabbi. She told him how Pinya

had neither eaten nor drunk for three days and nights and was just sitting there thinking, risking life and limb.

Whereupon the Rabbi called Gimpel and nine other of the foremost citizens of Helm and set out for Pinya's house.

When they arrived at the house, the Rabbi, Gimpel and the nine other Helmites saw that what Pinya's wife had reported was true: Pinya was indeed seated upon a stool in the middle of the room, his head propped on his hand, his brow wrinkled, his eyes glazed with a far-off look—truly thinking!

Said the Rabbi:

"Pinya, tell us what you are thinking about—maybe we can help you think your thought through to the end."

"No, no," replied Pinya, "not yet. It still isn't clear in my own mind. Let me think alone for another day."

"But, Pinya, you look pale and faint," said the Rabbi.

"No, no," replied Pinya, "I must have another day."

Said the Rabbi:

"Very well, we will leave you for another day."

On the morrow, the Rabbi, Gimpel and the other nine Helmites returned. Only the Rabbi spoke and he uttered but one word:

"Well?"

Again Pinya begged:

"Just one more day, Rabbi, one more day. I have not yet finished thinking."

Replied the Rabbi sternly:

"No, you must break your fast. You are risking your life and that is a sin. Stop thinking and have something to eat."

When the Rabbi commands, one must obey. So Pinya stopped thinking and sat down to eat. When he had finished, he became sleepy. He lay down. The Rabbi and the other Helmites remained, waiting for Pinya to wake. They were very curious to know what Pinya had been thinking about for so long.

When Pinya arose from his sleep, the Rabbi said to him:

"Well, Pinya, have a pinch of snuff and tell us what you were thinking about."

Replied Pinya:

"How can I tell when I didn't finish thinking?"

Said the Rabbi:

"Pinya, for four days and four nights you neither ate nor drank, but thought. True, you did not finish thinking. But surely it can't be a mere trifle that a man thinks about

for so long. You must have been thinking about something!"

Replied Pinya:

"Well, for four nights and four days I thought if all the men in the world became one huge man, and all the trees in the forests became one enormous tree, and all the rivers on the earth became one tremendous river and all the axes everywhere became one great axe—"

"Yes, yes?" asked the Helmites eagerly. "What then?"

Slowly Pinya went on:

"And if this giant of a man rose up and seized this great axe and struck a blow at this huge tree, just try and imagine—"

"Yes, yes! Go on!" urged the Helmites, hanging onto his every word.

"Imagine," said Pinya reflectively, stroking his curly little black beard, "imagine if this great tree with its long, thick branches, its millions and trillions of leaves, should topple into this tremendous river—how high would the splash be? Would it reach up to heaven, or even higher? You understand," and Pinya sighed mournfully, "I thought and thought and was just about to get the answer when you stopped me. Now all my thinking came to nought."

"Tsk! Tsk!" said the Helmites sympathetically.

Then Gimpel remarked:

"Now that's a brain for you! A veritable philosopher!"

So from that day on Pinya was known as Pinya the Philosopher.

And that is how it came to pass that when the Helmites were seeking a wise man to send to Warsaw to find out how fires were put out in that great city, they chose Pinya the Philosopher.

At the break of day Pinya awoke, recited his prayers, breakfasted, packed some food for the journey and set out for Warsaw.

Pinya walked. The road was dusty, the day was hot, and Pinya thought: A drink of cold water would surely be refreshing. But the road was long and dusty and there was no water.

So Pinya walked further. Soon he came to a hill. Pinya groaned and went on. Going uphill was hard. He climbed slowly, puffing and panting all the way to the top. On the hilltop it was cooler and nearby there was a little grove. In the grove, close to the road, stood a large shade tree. Underneath the tree was a big rock and from beneath the rock gushed a spring of clear cold water.

Pinya stopped, cast off his coat, wiped the sweat from his brow and sat down. Then he took a long drink from the icy spring, washed and ate. Growing sleepy, he took another drink from the spring, yawned slowly and murmured:

"To lie down in the shade of this tree would be pleasant. It is cool and comfortable here."

Making a pillow of his coat, he was soon ready for sleep. But Pinya was not called the Philosopher for nothing, and soon his shrewd brain posed a question:

"A fine thing! Here am I going to sleep, but when I awake, how will I know which way is Warsaw?"

Then Pinya had an idea: He took off his shoes and placed them out on the road with the toes pointing towards Warsaw. Now he could go safely to sleep and when he awoke, his shoes would tell him just which way to go. And without further ado, Pinya lay down and was soon fast asleep.

Not long afterwards, a stranger happened to pass, saw Pinya sleeping under the tree and noticed the shoes out in the middle of the road. They looked so funny standing there that, for no reason at all, the stranger just had to turn them around. Then he went on his way, whistling a merry tune.

Pinya the Philosopher slept long and soundly. When he awoke, he yawned contentedly and said to himself:

"God is good to me. I have eaten well, I have slept soundly and there are my shoes pointing the way to Warsaw. God is truly good to me."

He put on his shoes and continued on his way. One hour passed, then two, and suddenly he glimpsed a town in the distance. The first thing he saw was the cemetery and then there appeared the roofs of the houses. Pinya clucked his tongue and marvelled—from the distance Warsaw looked exactly like Helm. But Pinya was a Philosopher, and he reasoned:

"To be sure, isn't it written in the Great Books that the world is the same everywhere? Naturally, *that* is why Warsaw looks like Helm."

The nearer he approached the place, the more he marvelled. The streets looked exactly like the streets of Helm. Even the Town Baths looked the same. And an identical Town Hall. Why, there was a post for the watchman's

horse, just like the post near the Town Hall in Helm. And imagine, there in the middle of the marketplace stood a pear tree, just like in Helm. Pinya couldn't get over it. "True," he said to himself, "it is written that the world is the same everywhere, but I never expected it to be *so much* the same. That just goes to show you. When the Great Books say something, they know what they're talking about."

Pinya walked on. He gasped as he rounded the next corner. "Well, well, just such a street in Warsaw as my street in Helm." He continued walking. "Look, there is a house exactly the same as mine and standing just where mine does in Helm."

Pinya stood and stared and wondered. He stroked his curly little black beard and murmured: "Lo and behold, the whole world is like Helm."

And as he stood there, he heard a woman inside the house, shouting, "Moishe, stop that noise. Your father leaves and I think I'll get a little peace, so now *you* begin. Go bring in the goat. And don't say 'Later' or I'll—"

By this time Pinya was really impressed. Will God's wonders never cease? A scolding wife just like mine, nagging a disobedient son named Moishe, just like mine, in a house on a street just like mine. And imagine, as if all this

weren't wonder enough, this Moishe says "Later" when told to do something—just like mine.

Standing with mouth agape, he scrutinized the house, the porch, the gate, when suddenly out came his wife Zlota. When she saw Pinya, she clasped her hands in amazement and shrieked:

"Pinya, back so soon from Warsaw?"

Pinya nearly dropped from shock. How does this strange woman know that I am called Pinya and what does she mean when she says "Back so soon from Warsaw?" After all, I *am* in Warsaw.

When Zlota saw her Philosopher standing there with his mouth open wide enough for a cat to walk in, she began to scold:

"Why are you standing there like a dummy, staring at me with two glass eyes? Fool! Go to the Synagogue or you'll be late for evening prayers."

All his life Pinya had obeyed his wife Zlota. So now, without another thought, he obeyed this strange woman who was so much like his Zlota and went off to the Synagogue.

There, the Helmites greeted him with surprise and joy. After the services, they crowded around him, exclaiming:

"Back so soon? Now there's a messenger for you! Goes

to Warsaw in the morning and is back in Helm by evening!"

Pinya became very angry, but not being a Philosopher for nothing, he controlled himself and said calmly:

"I know that the Jews of Warsaw are clever but surely that doesn't give you the right to laugh at a stranger."

"Look here, Pinya," replied the Rabbi. "You may be a great Philosopher, but that's no reason for you to talk in riddles. Please tell us how they put out fires in Warsaw."

Spluttered Pinya:

"What are you talking about? I *am* in Warsaw!"

The Helmites became indignant. "Why are you making fun of us?" they cried. "You know you're back in Helm."

Still calm, Pinya answered:

"Jews of Warsaw, I am not called Pinya the Philosopher for nothing. I am in Warsaw and I have proof of it."

Whereupon Pinya told them how before he had gone to sleep, he had carefully placed his shoes on the road with the toes pointing towards Warsaw.

When the Helmites heard *this*, a hue and cry arose: if that's the case, then Pinya must be right and they are in Warsaw! A pretty kettle of fish! The women and children in Helm, and they, the men-folk, in Warsaw, all of a sudden! Something had to be done!

Once again timid Berel the Beadle spoke up in a piping voice, "I think I know how we can tell where we are. Remember how I painted *Zeh Hashul Shayech Lechelem, This Synagogue Belongs to Helm,* on the outside wall of the Synagogue. Let's go out and see if it's there. If it is, we're in Helm. If not, we're in Warsaw."

Being Berel's idea, it was naturally ridiculed, but the Helmites went out anyway. Happily, it was a bright, moonlit night, and sure enough there was the inscription on the Synagogue, clear and plain for everyone to see. It was as though a stone had been lifted from their hearts.

But not so with Pinya the Philosopher. He stood his ground, stroked his curly, red beard and asked:

"How can you explain the testimony of the shoes?"

At that moment they caught sight of their angry wives, coming to fetch them, as their suppers were getting cold. Then and there Berel the Beadle said:

"We must be in Helm—there can't be two sets of wives such as ours!"

And though it was against their better judgment to agree with the sentiments of Berel who was not quite wise in the measure of Helm, to this indeed they had to agree —there couldn't be two such sets of wives as theirs! Truly, it was certain they were in Helm!

Candles, radishes and garlic

THE PROBLEM OF HOW TO EXTIN-guish fires still beset the Helmites, so on the very next day they called a Town Meeting to choose a new messenger to send to Warsaw. They talked and talked, then talked some more and finally decided to send Shloime, for Shloime was a Scientist and a Scientist would know when a pair of shoes was turned around on the road. Shloime set out at once and arrived in Warsaw without mishap.

He walked about the broad streets of Warsaw and could not get enough of gazing at the large shops and staring at the tall, brick buildings. Everything was so beautiful it almost took his breath away. While wandering about as if entranced, he came upon a strange, high tower, encircled by a balcony. Shloime leaned back and stared up at the tower. On the balcony was a man wearing a

metal helmet, standing about doing nothing. The Scientist of Helm stopped a Warsaw Jew and asked:

"Tell me, good brother, why does that man stand up there on the balcony doing nothing?"

"He's protecting the city from fires," replied the other.

Shloime was overjoyed. This was just what he had come for. "How does he protect the city from fires?" he queried.

But the Warsaw Jew was no longer there. People in a big city are always in a hurry and this man was no exception.

Thought Shloime:

"Why bother people who are in a hurry? I'll climb up and ask the fellow himself."

So Shloime climbed up to the man on the tower and found him standing beside a big kettle-drum. Shloime inquired:

"Tell me, dear friend, I beg you, how do you protect Warsaw from fires?"

The man in the helmet, alone on the balcony day in and day out, was glad for a chance to chat with someone.

"Well, from this balcony, I can see all of Warsaw. I watch all day long and the moment I catch sight of a fire, I begin pounding on the kettle-drum."

"And then what?" implored Shloime excitedly. "Tell

me quickly! That's just what I've come all the way from Helm for."

When the man heard the word "Helm," he realized at once that he was not addressing someone with an ordinary mind, but one with the *superior* mental capacity of a Helmite. So, trying hard to keep from grinning, he replied:

"When I beat this kettle-drum, then and there the fire goes out."

Shloime gasped in amazement as he exclaimed: "Imagine! You beat on a kettle-drum here and the fire goes out there! Truly an unusual kettle-drum!"

"Aye, such is the power of this kettle-drum," rejoined the man in the helmet.

Whereupon Shloime blurted out:

"You must sell me the kettle-drum!"

Answered the man: "I need it here myself."

Said Shloime the Scientist:

"I'll give you one hundred gold-pieces."

When the man heard Shloime offer one hundred gold-pieces for an ordinary kettle-drum, he said to himself: "Now, take it easy, Yankel, don't seem too anxious, or the deal might be spoiled."

So, pretending reluctance, he said:

"I'll tell you what. Come back tomorrow morning and I'll see what I can do."

Early the very next day, Shloime returned and there was the kettle-drum, all ready and packed. Shloime was a little surprised that the man in the helmet seemed not at all dejected at the prospect of losing his unusual drum, but after all, that was none of his business. He quickly counted out the hundred gold-pieces and made his way back to Helm.

Back in Helm with the kettle-drum, Shloime excitedly called his townspeople together.

"Rejoice, O Helmites," he cried. "No more pails, no more buckets, no more running to the river for water every time a fire breaks out. At last all our problems are solved. Now all we have to do is beat on this kettle-drum and the fire will go out."

The people cheered. Never again would the scourge of fire threaten their beloved Helm. So, in the very center of the town, they erected a tall tower encircled by a balcony and put Shloime on it to stand there day in and day out and watch for fires.

Some weeks later, standing high on the tower, Shloime spied a thick, black cloud of smoke rising to the sky. Not

being a Scientist for nothing, his nimble brain reasoned thus: where there is smoke there must be fire, and without further ado, he seized the sticks and beat the kettle-drum.

The whole town came running. Shloime pounded on the kettle-drum as though his very life depended on it. But in spite of his drumming, red tongues of flame shot up through the smoke. Shloime drummed and the fire burned. He pounded harder and the fire burned stronger. He pounded so hard, he nearly split the drum, but another house took fire and then still another began to burn.

The Helmites stood and watched. True, Shloime was laboring faithfully. He drummed so hard he could barely catch his breath. But still they had to face the fact that the whole town would soon go up in smoke despite his drumming. So without even pausing to think—which, by the way, is what probably saved Helm that day—the Helmites seized their pails and buckets, ran down to the river and after hours of hauling water, finally managed to extinguish the flames.

After the fire, they called a Town Meeting and placed Shloime on trial. The Rabbi was the judge.

"Tell me, Shloime," queried the Rabbi. "You're supposed to be a Scientist, a man who should understand the burning of fires and the beating of kettle-drums. How is it that you let these two things get mixed up together?"

"Rabbi," replied Shloime earnestly. "With my own tongue I talked with the man in the helmet and with my own eyes I saw the kettle-drum and with my own ears I heard him beat on it. And now, I ask you, would they pay a man wages in Warsaw for doing nothing?"

The Rabbi hesitated, for this was indeed a good point. But after thinking hard for a few hours, he thought up this question:

"Then pray tell me why did not the kettle-drum work here in Helm?"

Now Shloime had to pause, for this too was not a bad point. So after *he* thought hard for several hours, he thought up this reply:

"It is not for nothing that I am known as Shloime the Scientist. After careful deliberation, I have come to the conclusion that if the drum worked in Warsaw, it should work in Helm. That is the nature of the laws of science."

The Rabbi took a pinch of snuff and said:

"Then, tell me, worthy Scientist, why did we have to haul water to put out the fire?"

"That is a good question," observed Shloime. "And for the answer, I recommend that we send a committee of ten citizens to Warsaw."

Which was what they did.

On the morrow the ten Helmites set out for Warsaw. All day they travelled and towards evening they sighted the tall buildings of Warsaw in the distance. Said one of the ten to the other nine:

"It will soon be dark. What is the point of arriving in a strange city at night? Let us stop at the nearest inn instead."

The nine Helmites nodded approval to the other one.

The emissaries presented themselves at the nearest inn and said to the innkeeper:

"We wish to have supper and lodging for the night."

"I have enough food for the ten of you," replied the innkeeper, "but not enough beds."

"That's all right," responded the Helmites, "after all we're not princes—we can sleep on the floor."

After a good supper and a leisurely grace, the ten Helmites went upstairs where the innkeeper had spread

a bed of straw on the floor for his guests. Before going to sleep, they instructed him not to fail to wake them at daybreak.

Bright and early the next morning the innkeeper knocked at their door and shouted:

"Helmites, awake! It's daylight already."

They stirred, yawned noisily and called out:

"Thank you! We'll be right down."

The innkeeper descended the stairs, went out into the barn, drove his cows into the pasture, went back to the barn, fed the chicks and geese, hitched his horse to the wagon, drove to town, bought a calf and then returned to the inn.

When he went upstairs to clean out the straw, lo and behold, there were the Helmites still lying stretched out on the floor.

"Good Lord," he exclaimed. "You begged me to wake you at daybreak because you wanted to get to Warsaw early in the morning. Now look what time it is and you're still lying there like lazy good-for-nothings."

"No, no!" cried the Helmites. "Don't you see what a terrible thing has happened to us? We tangled our legs together while we slept and now we cannot untangle them. Save us, O worthy innkeeper."

"But why don't you just stand up?" he exclaimed in amazement.

"How can we?" they rejoined. "We don't know whose feet are whose and how can we stand up on someone else's feet?"

"Woe is me!" sighed the innkeeper. "I guess I forgot that I was dealing with Helmites."

"Save us, save us!" they continued to cry.

"Very well, I'll save you. But you'll have to pay me for my pains."

"We'll pay you, we'll pay you, we'll pay you well," they shouted.

The innkeeper left the room for a moment, soon returned with a long, fat, heavy leather whip and with it, began flogging their naked legs.

As though boiling water had been poured upon them, the Helmites jumped up, and wonder of wonders, each one stood on his own pair of legs. Stroking their aching limbs and with tears in their eyes, they thanked the innkeeper, dressed hurriedly, said their prayers and left for Warsaw.

After arriving in Warsaw, it did not take them long to find the tower. Craning their necks, they looked up. Aye,

III

Shloime the Scientist had reported scientifically. High up on the tower was a circular balcony on which a man with a helmet stood beside a kettle-drum.

All ten climbed slowly and laboriously to the top of the tower to have a talk with the man. He gave them the same story he had given Shloime: as soon as he caught sight of a fire anywhere in the city he would begin to beat the drum and the fire would go out.

Queried the Helmites:

"Then will you explain this to us: our Shloime bought a kettle-drum from you for a hundred gold-pieces and when a fire broke out in our town, he drummed and drummed but the fire would not go out until we began pouring water on it."

Replied the man:

"O, didn't I tell him? In addition to the kettle-drum, you also need a fire-engine with a long rubber hose, a pump, barrels of water and helmets for the firemen. I must have forgotten."

"O, is that all that was wrong?" exclaimed the Helmites, delighted that it was nothing more serious. Then they thanked him profusely and left.

They immediately hastened to a company which sold fire-engines and after careful deliberation, they selected

a beautiful machine with big brass handles and a long rubber hose. At one end of the hose, there was an elaborately fashioned spraying nozzle and at the other a sturdy pump. They were also careful not to forget helmets for the firemen.

When the dealer realized that these people were Helmites, he said:

"Do you also want these barrels filled to the brim with the best Warsaw fire-fighting water, all ready for use? We have a special sale on them today."

"The best is none too good for us," they replied gratefully. "Send them along."

The happy Helmites returned home and soon there followed the shining new engine, the rubber hose, the pump, the helmets and twenty iron-rimmed barrels filled with the Warsaw water. The townsfolk crowded around and clucked their tongues as they examined this new wonder. The burnished brass shone like gold in the sun. It was a dazzling sight to behold. Every one agreed that with such a fire-engine, no fire would stand a chance in Helm.

To house their new treasure they built a handsome fire-station and gave Berel the Beadle still another job—keeping guard over it. Then fifteen burly firemen were carefully selected and specially appointed by Mottel the Mayor.

Some weeks later a fire broke out in Helm and Shloime began pounding the drum for all he was worth. This time his efforts did not go unrewarded. Dashing to the fire-station, the firemen seized their brass helmets, grabbed their equipment and before you could say "Berel the Beadle," there they were at the scene of the fire—engine, rubber hose, pump, nozzle and all. Not forgetting the twenty barrels of special Warsaw fire-fighting water—not the Helmites.

In no time at all, the Warsaw water was spraying the fire and barrel after barrel was bravely doing its duty. Then suddenly, the stream of gushing water drooped and ceased altogether with Feivel the Fire-Chief left standing there like a simpleton holding the empty nozzle in his hands.

"More water!" shouted Feivel. "Another barrel!" But quickly came the mournful reply, "That was our last barrel of special Warsaw fire-fighting water." This was indeed a calamity. No more Warsaw water and the fire still raging.

Mottel the Mayor hurriedly called a Town Meeting and the Helmites began to argue about the water situation— whether to send for more Warsaw water or whether the

ordinary Helm water would do in a pinch. Luckily, in the meantime, Berel the Beadle had organized a bucket brigade and put the fire out.

For a long time after that there were no fires in Helm. Alone on his balcony, Shloime with wrinkled brow could sit and *science* from morning till night without anything or anyone disturbing him. Feivel the Fire-Chief and his fifteen burly firemen drew their wages and dozed all day. As he kept guard over the fire-station, Berel the Beadle tended his garden and grew his vegetables.

But alack and alas, this state of affairs was too good to last. One day another fire broke out in Helm and everybody sprang into action. Quickly, all the fire-fighting equipment was hauled to the burning house. The firemen began pumping—pumping with all their might. But not a drop of water came out of the hose.

The house blazed away. The firemen pumped harder. Still no water. The house burned like a torch soaked in kerosene. The firemen outdid themselves. But not a trickle came out of the nozzle.

"Something must be wrong with the fire-engine!" cried Feivel as he ran to examine it. Sure enough, inside he found stumps of candles, radishes and garlic.

Feivel was furious and demanded to know who was responsible for this terrible thing.

"They're mine," replied Berel the Beadle, "and I've been looking for them everywhere. Please return them to me."

"Indeed I won't," retorted Feivel angrily. "All because of them this house is going to go up in flames."

Berel hauled Feivel to the Rabbi, claiming that, as is customary with Beadles everywhere, he needed the little extra money he could eke out on the side by selling his candles, radishes and garlic—the candles to students of the Talmud who studied late into the night, the radishes to the women for their Friday night *gefilte* fish and the garlic for medicine to one and all when they had the bellyache. Even to Feivel, he added.

Feivel interrupted: "Then why did you have to keep them in the fire-engine?"

"Where then could I hide them without the children finding them? You know, Rabbi, what would happen to me without my candles, radishes and garlic. And the fire-engine is my only hiding place," pleaded Berel.

"Very well," said the Rabbi, "let it be your hiding place but Helm must have its fire-engine to put out fires. So my decision is that three days before every fire, you must be notified by Feivel the Fire-Chief whereupon you

must remove your candles, radishes and garlic from the fire-engine."

Both Feivel the Fire-Chief and Berel the Beadle were delighted with the Rabbi's compromise and departed in good spirits to assist in clearing away the cinders of the house that had burnt to the ground.

Time passed and there were many fires in Helm, but no matter how hard he tried, Feivel never quite managed to know when a fire would break out until it actually did. Thus, of course, he could never notify Berel three days ahead of time, thus the Beadle's candles, radishes and garlic were never disturbed in their perfect hiding-place, and thus, till this very day, fires are extinguished in Helm in the good old-fashioned way.

A cat comes to Helm

119

YEARS PASSED BUT HELM WAS STILL HELM. Nothing had changed. In the center of town the great Synagogue still stood, and near the Synagogue was the shining fire-engine guarded by Berel the Beadle. There in front of the Town Hall stood the post where the night watchman tied his horse, and high on the mountain-top the sails of the mill turned proudly in the wind.

Things were as of old, and life had become easy for the Helmites. Everything was orderly now, everything was done according to custom.

For instance, when a Helmite had to have a letter written, it was customary for him to go to a little red table that stood near the Synagogue. On a tall stool beside the table sat Simcha the Scribe. Always, the first question Simcha would ask a client was:

"Is this letter going to a deaf man?"

If it was going to a deaf man, Simcha would be careful to write in great, big letters.

There were many other things that had once been problems in Helm but had since been solved in true Helmite fashion. There was the case of Berel the Beadle. As Berel grew older, his health became poorer. Now, taking up a great part of his little home were hundreds of wooden window shutters. Thus, whenever he became ill, he didn't have to leave his sick-bed and go out into the cold streets at dawn to knock on the shutters and wake the towns-people for the morning service. Without even leaving the house, he could knock on every shutter in town.

There was also a large wooden table that cluttered up Berel's home. This was only used during the winter-time, after a snow-fall. When Berel trudged through the streets to awaken the townsfolk he would always soil the beautiful snow. This was a shame, said the Helmites. Something had to be done. So Gimpel made this brilliant suggestion: after every snowfall, let four Helmites come to Berel's house, seat him on the table and carry him through the town. So it was done and henceforth Berel the Beadle never trampled the fresh, white, newly fallen snow.

Then there was the wooden fence that stood near the court-yard of the Synagogue. Two small, round holes were cut in the fence. These holes were the Town Prison. When a culprit was to be punished, he had to put his arms

through the two holes. Then two barrel hoops were placed in his hands. Thus, no guard was needed, for no man, no matter how strong, could pull the large, iron hoops through the small holes. The offender just had to stand there till the hoops were taken from his hands.

Not far from the prison there were two high poles from which hung a pair of brightly lit lanterns. Across the poles was nailed a large sign reading "All Searching Done Here." You see, whenever the Helmites lost anything at night, it was very difficult to find it in the dark. So here, for the convenience of the townspeople were these two brightly lit lanterns where they could immediately come to look for the lost article in comfort. This made searching a pleasure.

Such were the customs and institutions of the wise men of Helm where life had been made orderly and everything was thought out in advance. But one day when a horde of mice suddenly descended upon the town, they became a problem for which the Helmites could find no solution in their books of customs and institutions.

Nobody knew where the mice came from. But they surely made the lives of the Helmites miserable, for these mice were not like ordinary mice who skulk in the dark, hide in little holes and timidly nibble at scraps of food

when no one is about. The Helm mice were indeed un-usual. Fearlessly, they walked about in broad daylight and were even seen promenading through the Town Square in pairs. They also made themselves at home in all the houses of Helm and even invaded the mansion of leading citizen Gimpel. They came to the table at meal time and had a way of gobbling up all the food the moment it was set out.

A pretty kettle of mice! For many moons there had been no need to call a Town Meeting but now there was nothing else to be done. All Helm flocked to the meeting, fathers and mothers, sons and daughters, and even a grandchild or two. They thought and thought till they could think no more—then they thought a little longer. While all this was going on, Berel the Beadle, finding the air in the Town Hall stuffy from so much brilliant thinking, wandered out.

He wandered up to the mill on the mountaintop. Sit-ting in the doorway of the mill there was the miller, and at his feet was a strange, furry animal, sunning itself. Suddenly the animal rose and stretched and Berel noticed its long, fine whiskers, its sharp nails and burning green eyes.

"What is it?" he asked the miller.

"A cat," was the reply. "I have it to keep the mice away from the mill."

Berel gasped with joy, 'Give me that wonderful cat."

Soon afterwards, Berel returned to the Town Hall carrying the cat in his arms.

"This may sound foolish," he said, "but I've heard that every time the cat looks at a mouse, the mouse drops dead. I think it must be something coming from the cat's eyes that does it."

Everybody laughed aloud at this silly idea but just then a couple of mice entered the Hall—probably to attend the meeting. They caught sight of the cat, turned on their heels and ran like mad. The cat, on the other hand, upon spying the mice, leaped out of Berel's hands and dashed after them.

The Helmites were impressed. This cat must be truly a brave and noble creature that the wicked mice tremble and fly before it. After a few weeks, there wasn't a mouse to be found in Helm for love or money. The gratitude of the people was so great that nothing was too good for the cat.

They built a special house for it, furnished it with the finest goose down and supplied the cat with the most flavorsome delicacies. Soon however a new problem arose for

they discovered that it had an enormous appetite. No matter how much food they brought, the cat was still hungry.

In their anxiety to appease their benefactor, the Helmites emptied their pantries. But so far, not so good. The cat consumed mountains of food. To keep it content, they were even forced to raid the grocery stores in the middle of the night. Finally, things became so serious that a Town Meeting was called where it was proclaimed that the cat was just as bad as the mice and would have to be exiled from Helm. So they issued an edict exiling the cat from Helm and read it to her. To no avail! The cat calmly disregarded the order and went on her way, eating the Helmites out of house and home. The Helmites suffered. Still it was better to suffer from one cat than from hordes of mice!

Until one day things became desperate. The cat had sauntered into the kitchen of Yentil, wife of Mottel the Mayor, just as she was sitting down to a bite of food. The cat marched itself up to the cream pitcher, uncovered it, gobbled up the cream and licked the pitcher clean, then looked around for something more. It seems that when a cat is hungry, it's hungry.

Just then it spied a slice of cheese in Yentil's hand and pounced on the woman, but Yentil jumped away. Now

the cat wheeled round and sunk its sharp teeth into her hand. Yentil tried to seize the cat by the scruff of the neck but the cat fell upon the good woman, scratching her face and throwing her to the floor. Yentil screamed. The cat became excited and sprang into the cupboard, breaking all the special Passover dishes with a crash. The screams and the noise brought Mottel running. He tried to catch the cat, but it sprang through the open window and disappeared. Go capture the wind!

A Town Meeting was quickly called and the cat was put on trial. Mottel refused to be the judge. He might be partial, he argued. After all, the injured woman was his wife. The Rabbi presided and the cat was sentenced to death. It was decided that Berel the Beadle would take the cat to the roof of the Synagogue, hold it before him with both hands and jump off the roof. Berel would fall on top of the cat, crush it to death and the town would be rid of the evil beast.

The next day, with the cat in his arms, Berel climbed onto the roof of the Synagogue to carry out the sentence. But even the best laid plans of mice and men often go astray and though Berel the Beadle jumped off the roof— seriously spraining his ankle, by the way—the cat sprang away as Berel jumped.

The Helmites chased the cat but it crawled onto the adjoining rooftop. A nimble lad crawled out after it whereupon the cat jumped across to the next roof.

A Town Meeting was called on the spot and it was decided to set fire to the house on which the cat was lurking. True, the house would be burned to the ground but at least the cat would also perish.

And so the Helmites set fire to the house. The walls took fire nicely and then the roof. But as soon as the flames began licking at the cat's tail, what did it do but jump to the next roof. Not wishing to waste a house with nothing accomplished, the order was quickly given to set fire to the next house too. And it was so done. But lo, the cat jumped to another roof. Nothing daunted, the torch was applied to the third house. But the cat was strong and did not tire easily. It jumped to still another roof but the Helmites had made their decision and nothing would stop them from carrying it out. The cat must be destroyed!

Before the sun had set that night, all Helm was burned to the ground—not a stick or a stone had been left uncharred, but what did that matter when it was pretty certain that the cat had not escaped to Shedlitz, as some people said.

Who knows, maybe you're a Helmite too!

IT WAS AFTER THE CALAMITOUS FIRE THAT A law was passed making it a crime to utter the word *cat* in Helm. For a disaster such as the one caused by the c - t had never been visited upon the town before.

Surveying the charred ruins, the Helmites bemoaned their fate. Then the Rabbi spoke up:

"My poor, suffering brethren, do not grieve. Just remember how crowded the Synagogue had become and how we were always wanting to push out the walls and make it bigger. Now we can build a new Synagogue as big as Gimpel's potato patch. And as for our homes, weren't you all sick and tired of coming back to the same old rooms, the same old walls and the same old furniture? Now we can rebuild to our heart's content without the trouble of tearing down a thing. Truly, the fire was a blessing in disguise for which we should give thanks to God."

So then and there the groans departed from the lips of the Helmites, the furrows left their brows and a light came into their eyes. They began singing praises to the Lord. Berel the Beadle either failed to say his prayers in full or raced through them in a hurry, for the others were still swaying gently back and forth with eyes half closed when he piped up:

"True, it was a happy day on which that unmentionable animal came to Helm, but pray tell me, O wise Rabbi, where will we get the money for all this rebuilding?"

"Very simply," interrupted Gimpel. "It is well known that our brethren throughout the world have kind hearts and open hands. They will help us. I myself, with Mottel the Mayor and Pinya the Philosopher, will go to Warsaw to tell them what has befallen us."

So said, so done. They left that very day.

Being descendants of the great Patriarch Abraham who was renowned for his generosity, the Warsaw Jews gave fully to their stricken brothers. And soon the leading citizens of Helm had collected a goodly sum of money and without delay, set out for home.

That night, sitting in an inn, the three Helmites were sipping strong, hot tea from tall, thin glasses and listening to the tales of the other travellers crowded around the table. Helmites love to hear stories of exciting adventure but the yarns that assailed the ears of Gimpel, Mottel and Pinya curdled their blood and made their hair stand on

end. The travelling merchants, egged on by the effect they were having on our three Helmites, soon were outdoing one another in making up fantastic tales about bandits, highwaymen and murderers.

Before long, Gimpel, Mottel and Pinya had turned white as chalk and were quaking in their boots. Going quickly up to their room, they called a special meeting to discuss the seriousness of their situation. For here they were, carrying a fortune in gold and convinced that the money would be stolen and their throats cut before they reached the next town. A pretty kettle of worries!

Hour after hour they thought and thought and finally when dawn broke the next morning, together, as though by magic, all three hit upon the same idea—they would buy feathers! They would take all the money and buy feathers. Why feathers, some simple-minded reader might ask. Obviously, that reader is not as quick as our Helmites. You see, feathers are light. With the money, they would buy hundreds and hundreds of sacksful. [Now if the money were stolen, it could easily be concealed by thieves, but nobody, not even the cleverest highwayman, could hide hundreds of sacks full of feathers.] Thus, they would bring the feathers to Helm, sell them and with the money, rebuild the town. Not so dumb, our Helmites, eh?

Forgetting all about their lost sleep, the three Helmites hastened back to Warsaw and before the day was over, there wasn't a single pound of feathers to be had in the city. Gimpel and his companions had bought them all.

After ridding themselves of their last kopek they began preparing for the journey home when they came upon a new worry: Here they were with tons and tons of feathers and no way of getting them to Helm. A pretty kettle of feathers! To hire wagons, horses and drivers would cost more money than the feathers themselves were worth, and besides the Helmites had no money left. Then what was to be done?

Again they thought and thought and again their thinking was not in vain. As a matter of fact, delighted, they were sure that no one had ever had such a remarkable

idea before. Feathers are light, they reasoned. Feathers can be carried by the wind. When the next strong wind blew in the direction of Helm, they would open the sacks and release the feathers into the wind. Quickly the feathers would be blown to Helm, high in the air, out of the reach of bandits, highwaymen and murderers—and besides not a kopek spent for transportation!

Soon a favorable wind arrived. The Helmites quickly ripped open the sacks, released the feathers and as the swirling white cloud darkened the sun, they could not stop slapping each other on the back for the way they had out-witted the thieves. Then, happy as birds, they departed for Helm.

The entire town came out to meet the returning travelers. A Town Meeting was called on the spot and the Rabbi requested that the three leading citizens tell everything that had happened on their long journey.

Gimpel related how everywhere they went they had been received with the greatest hospitality. They collected a handsome sum of money, enough to rebuild every house in the town, a Town Hall, a Town Bath and even a new Synagogue, twice as large as the one they had before.

All the people rejoiced. Cheers arose for the heroes,

Gimpel, Mottel and Pinya. In a moment of quiet, the Rabbi politely remarked: "Should we not put the gold in a safe place now?"

"O, we do not have the gold," replied Mottel.

"You mean you've been robbed?" cried the frightened Rabbi.

"Oh no," rejoined Gimpel, "not us. The money is out of harm's way. We were afraid to risk journeying with so much gold, so we bought feathers and let them travel safely in a high wind that was blowing towards Helm."

When the townspeople heard this, they chuckled with glee. What an extraordinary way of outwitting thieves! They congratulated each other on having had the good sense to send their wisest men on this mission. Only Berel the Beadle murmured words of protest:

"True, this was a brilliant plan to prevent robbery, but to whom are we going to sell all these feathers when they get here?"

But by now the Helmites had learned to pay no attention to Berel, except when they needed him to perform some unpleasant task.

Finally, Berel's youngest son, Shmerel, who was only four years old, chirped up impudently:

"Where are the feathers? Why haven't they come yet? Doesn't the wind travel faster than people?"

Gimpel answered the saucy lad, for Gimpel's greatness lay not alone in his wisdom but also in his noble humility:

"When you grow up, Shmerel, and get some sense into that childish brain of yours, you'll understand that if a man can sometimes be late, surely feathers can also be late."

So the Helmites waited a day, two days, a week, two weeks—but not a feather arrived. A Town Meeting was called and the messengers were again questioned:

"Weeks have passed since you returned," said the Rabbi somewhat impatiently, "and not a single feather has come."

Replied Pinya:

"But don't you remember, Rabbi, that it was raining a few weeks ago. The feathers must have gotten wet. We must give them a chance to get dry. Wet feathers cannot be carried by the wind—everyone knows that."

"True," replied the Helmites, "very true. We must wait."

So they waited another week, and another and another until months went by. Not a solitary sign of the feathers!

The Rabbi, terribly worried, thought and thought. He

took a pinch of snuff, sneezed, then took another and sneezed again. It was no use. Finally, in desperation, he appealed to Gimpel for help. That worthy citizen, without snuff or sneezing, suddenly realized what had happened. Trembling with excitement, he exclaimed:

"Of course! Why didn't we think of it before? The feathers have gone astray. Being *strangers* they didn't know where Helm was."

"Then what shall we do now?" the anxious Helmites clamored.

"Simple," replied Gimpel. "Let us send out our own feathers to find the foreign feathers and show them the way to Helm."

Then all the Helmites went to their homes, ripped open their pillows, featherbeds and quilts and let the feathers fly away with the wind to find the foreign feathers and show them the way to Helm.

Months passed but the foreign feathers did not arrive nor did the Helmite feathers return. That was bad, very bad, especially since winter was approaching. The women began to whimper and the men to weep. A Town Meeting was called and the Rabbi arose:

"Helmites, why do you grieve? Surely, what must be, must be. True, our homes were burned but did we not get rid of the cat? Likewise, Gimpel, Mottel and Pinya did buy feathers with the money for our new homes. But aren't they our leading citizens? Shouldn't we be grateful that their throats weren't cut? And true, the foreign feathers did get lost in the wind but didn't that save transportation costs? Then, too, our Helmite feathers were sent out to find them but—"

Here the Rabbi paused a moment and then exclaimed:

"But surely it cannot be for nothing that not even a lonely feather is left in Helm. My people, the Lord works in mysterious ways his wonders to perform. This is a sign from on high. Like the destruction of Jerusalem in ancient times, the destruction of Helm is a sign that we must go out into the world and spread the wisdom that is our heritage and tradition. Like our forefathers of old, let us go forth with courage in our hearts to fulfill our destiny!"

And that is what the Helmites did. Not with sorrow and not with tears, but proudly, they went forth from Helm and dispersed over the face of the earth. They mingled with all the peoples of the world and dutifully spread the wisdom that was once the pride of Helm alone. And so, dear reader, if you discover a bit of the Helmite in yourself, you'll know the reason why.

HERE ENDETH THE STORY
OF THE WISE MEN
OF HELM